MURDER AT HARTIGAN HOUSE

A Ginger Gold Mystery
Book 2

la
plume
PRESS

Lee Strauss

Ginger **Gold Mysteries**
(in order)
Murder on the SS Rosa
Murder at Hartigan House
Murder at Bray Manor

Murder at Hartigan House
A Ginger Gold Mystery
Book 2
By Lee Strauss
Cover by Steven Novak Illustrations
Copyright © 2017
ISBN: **978-1-988677-04-0**

Published by La Plume Press

CHAPTER ONE

GINGER GOLD hesitated at the front door of Hartigan House. She hadn't expected to feel anything, but instead she shouldered a heavy shawl of melancholy. This grand, three-storey structure built of limestone, situated in the picturesque Kensington street of Mallowan Court, had grown tired over the war years. The stones greyer, the garden wilder. The house had been her home for the first eight years of her life. The last time she'd visited had been a decade earlier on her honeymoon.

Her mostly happy childhood was long gone as was her lovely husband.

Haley Higgins, Ginger's good friend and travelling companion, noticed her disquietude. "Is everything all right?"

"Hartigan House holds a lot of memories." Ginger was torn in her allegiances: London the place of her birth or Boston the place where she came of age. She'd lived in the brownstone on Beacon Hill for over twenty-two years, yet England was etched deeply in her soul.

And now, to finally return—it was with this disconcerting welcome. A telegram received while on board the SS *Rosa*: GHASTLY DISCOVERY IN ATTIC OF HARTIGAN HOUSE.

Ginger, rousing her inner strength, stepped to the front door and engaged the wrought iron knocker.

"This is your house, isn't it?" Haley said. A lock of long, curly brown hair escaped its faux bob, and she pushed it behind her ear. "Surely you don't have to knock?"

"I'm not in possession of a key and I'm quite certain the door is locked."

Haley tested the knob and found Ginger's prediction to be true.

Ginger adjusted her yellow cloche hat, trimmed with blue ribbon to match her fine linen suit purchased on 5th Avenue in New York and patted her red bob with gloved hands. Her Boston terrier Boss waited obediently by her feet.

Their arrival was expected. Ginger had telegrammed the details of her journey before leaving Boston, and the door soon opened. Standing before them was Mr. Pippins, the butler. The years seemed to have caught up with him. His shoulders slumped slightly, and his hair had all but disappeared. But his eyes remained their bright cornflower-blue, and they twinkled as he stared back at her.

"My dear Lady Gold." He spoke her name with a slight quiver, giving away the emotion he experienced at seeing her. A dramatic image flashed through Ginger's mind: a scrawny redheaded girl held firmly by her father's strong hands as she wept, her eyes locking with her beloved butler as her father took her away.

A tear escaped from the corner of her eye, and she threw herself into his arms. "Oh, Pips."

Clive Pippins, stiffening at first to this unorthodox greeting, returned the embrace. Ginger released her hold, stepped back, and clasped her hands in front of her. She sensed Pippins' embarrassment and shared in it. There were proper ways to do things, especially in England, and showing overt affection to a member of one's staff was *not* proper. She cleared her throat and smiled. "It's so good to see you again, Pips."

Pippins stood tall, hands relaxed behind his back. "My sympathies, once again, on the loss of your father. Mr. Hartigan was a good man."

"Thank you." Ginger desperately missed her father, but seeing Pippins and knowing his devotion to her helped to ease some of the pain.

Ginger glanced at Haley who stood expectantly in her brown tweed suit and sturdy Oxford heels. "Oh, my manners. Pippins, this is my good friend Miss Higgins."

Pippins bowed. "Madam."

"How do you do, Mr. Pippins," Haley said with her noticeable Boston accent. She reached out her hand, her eyes crinkling at the corners as she smiled. "I'm a commoner."

Pippins' lips twitched in amusement. He accepted her hand with a sturdy shake.

"Miss Higgins was Father's nurse for the last three years," Ginger said. "She's come to London to study at the London School of Medicine for Women." Ginger linked her arm to Haley's. "She's going to be a doctor!"

Pippins nodded agreeably. "How wonderful."

Ginger swooped up her Boston terrier and patted his black head affectionately. "And this is Boss. Short for Boston."

"A fine-looking specimen, madam. How was your journey?"

"Quite lovely," Ginger said. "Apart from a short but fierce storm, the weather was pleasant." She omitted the news about the murder onboard the SS *Rosa* and the part she and Haley played in solving it.

Ginger finally had a chance to take in the foyer. Black and white tiled floor, a large chandelier that hung from the height of the second level, windows on either side of the double-panelled front doors that added natural light. The formidable areca palm plants in large ceramic pots hailing from India, once lined up along the base of the stairwell were missing—much to be expected when a house has been shut up for so many years.

"We don't have a footman, madam," Pippins said, "but I'd be happy to bring your things in."

Pippins, a confirmed bachelor, had to be in his seventies now, and Ginger didn't intend to burden him with such a laborious task. "That's quite all right, Pips. I've arranged for our things to be transported here by motor-van. The driver will be able to manage."

"Yes, madam."

Ginger eyed him wistfully. "I don't suppose you could call me 'Little Miss'?" Little Miss had been Pippins' pet name for her when she was a child. He was the only staff member to take time to entertain her. Subtle games like I spy and noughts and crosses (what Haley would call X's and O's)—never when her father was around, or in the presence of other staff as that would be unseemly for a member of staff. Her heart squeezed with the nostalgia.

"Little Miss, madam?" His eyes flickered with the memory, and he smiled. "I think not, madam."

Ginger let out a playful sigh. The pet name didn't suit a thirty-year-old woman anyway.

"Can I bring you some tea, madam?" Pippins asked. "After the train ride from Liverpool, you must be worn out."

"Tea sounds marvellous, Pips, but first we must know what your urgent, mysterious message is all about," she said referring to the telegram. Her curiosity was greater than her desire to put her feet up. Besides, she'd had a good sleep at the inn they'd stayed overnight at in Liverpool, and currently didn't feel all that tired. "I take it you've found something distasteful?"

"I believe he used the word, ghastly," Haley said. "Such a strong word. I'm dying to know what it is."

Pippins' expression turned grave. "It *is* rather ghastly, so do prepare yourself. Please follow me." A wide staircase circled up to the second floor, which horseshoed around the foyer giving the entrance its grand high ceiling. At the end of the passage was a door used by the servants to access the second floor. It opened to a small landing with steep steps that went down to the kitchen and up to the attic where the staff sleeping quarters were found. Rooms for women were in the west wing and the men's rooms to the east.

"I do apologise for bringing you into the servants' quarters, madam."

"It's quite all right, Pips."

Ginger's hope was that the problem in the attic was something trivial like dry rot or black mould. She wondered why Pippins hadn't taken it upon himself to ring for repairs. Perhaps, since he was newly back to Hartigan House and answered now to her instead of her father, he no longer felt he had the authority to make such calls on his own.

"I'm filled with curiosity, Pippins," Ginger said. "Do give us a clue."

Pippins hesitated then said. "I'm really at a loss how to describe it."

"Can we pause for a breather," Haley said, stopping midway up the step. "I am out of shape."

"I'm no better," Ginger said. "Pippins is bringing us to shame."

Pippins puffed out his chest with pride. "Years of going up and down daily, madam."

Ginger laughed. "Perhaps we should take rooms up here, Haley."

Pippins instantly turned serious. "Absolutely not, madam."

Before Ginger could explain that she wasn't serious, Pippins marched down the passage in the men's quarters to the very last room at the end. He removed a key from his pocket. "A skeleton key, madam," he explained. "Opens all the attic doors."

The lock clicked and the door swung open.

As Ginger reached the threshold, she couldn't keep a gasp of horror from escaping her lips.

Oh mercy!

In the middle of the room, lying on the floor, was a decomposed body.

CHAPTER TWO

GINGER HAD SEEN her fair share of gruesome remains during the war, but still the sight of the bones on the floor in her house was shocking. "Who is it?"

"I wish I knew, madam," Pippins said.

The small room was sparsely decorated with only a narrow bed up against the short wall and a wooden chest of drawers, coated in dust, against the taller wall. Haley approached the skeletal remains and gave them a cursory examination.

"The corpse is in dry decay. Pelvic bones indicate the victim is female, however we could surmise that by the dress. It appears the right hand is missing its distal phalanx."

"The finger tip?" Ginger said. "What could've

happened to it?"

"It's hard to say." She wrinkled her nose in contemplation. "I can't be 100 percent sure, but I'd say these remains are at least ten years old."

"Hartigan House was shut up ten years ago," Ginger said, "which means the body was here when that happened." She turned to Pippins who waited quietly by the door. "Pippins, how is it possible that this woman wasn't discovered at that time?"

Pippins regarded her with a look of discomfort. "I'm afraid, madam, the door had been locked. We had a telegram from Mr. Hartigan, not to go inside."

Mr. Hartigan? Ginger's eyelashes fluttered at the implication. "My father?"

Pippins nodded. "You can understand why I haven't gone to the police. I'm eager to keep rumours out of the tabloids. In fact, no one else in this house, besides the three of us, knows."

"I appreciate your discretion," Ginger said. The last thing she wanted was for her father's good name to be dragged through the mud. The idea that he had somehow been involved in the demise of this woman sat like a boulder on her chest. She swallowed to push down the dread. "You did the right thing, Pippins."

"Perhaps her clothes might be a clue to her identity," Haley said.

The flattened red evening gown that was draped over the bones had been savagely attacked by moths, leaving damaging holes in their wake. Ginger squatted next to Haley and stroked the fabric carefully. "It's a Lucile," she

---

11

said.

"A what?" Haley asked.

"The dress is a Lucile, an haute couture design by Lady Duff-Gordon."

"How do you know that?"

"Lady Duff-Gordon has shops in New York. I recognise the lines. Creamy satin draping to the floor and a second shorter layer angling over the top from one hip. The contrasting black empire waist bodice, with matching silk bow pinned on the right side. You're right about the timeline. This dress is about ten years old. I used to own a similar one myself."

"Do you think the victim is from New York?" Haley asked.

"Not necessarily. The House of Lucile originated in London."

"An evening gown would suggest she was at Hartigan House as a guest, would it not?" Haley said. "She must have been reported missing."

Ginger conceded. "Yes, I suspect the police will be quick to identify her."

Boss crawled under the bed and returned, fur covered in dust.

"Boss!" Ginger said. "Look how filthy you are now."

"He has something in his mouth," Haley said. She knelt and held out a palm. "Whatcha got there, ol' boy?"

Boss released his findings and sat, his stub of a tail shimmering against the dusty wooden floor.

"What is it?" Ginger asked.

"It looks like the missing phalanx."

"How did it get under the bed?"

"Rats?"

Ginger's stomach clenched. A body lying in Hartigan House for over a decade? This was bad, very bad indeed.

"I'd like to know how she ended up in the men's quarters." Ginger said. She faced the butler. "Pippins, who last slept in this room?"

"These quarters were last occupied by Mr. Andrew Bailey."

"Father's valet?" Ginger groaned inwardly. She wished she could go to her father and demand an explanation, but alas, she could not. She would have to unearth this mystery, and her father's alleged involvement, on her own. "Let's not breathe a word of this for now."

"Ginger," Haley said. "You can't lock the door and pretend this murder didn't happen. She has family somewhere wondering about her. This has to be reported."

"Oh, Haley, I know you're right, but can we wait a day?" Ginger said. She needed time to think this through.

Haley sighed. "She's been here for ten years. I suppose one more day won't hurt."

The chime from the front door sounded a peal that was loud enough to be heard on the third floor. "That will be our luggage," Ginger said to Pippins. "Would you mind showing the driver in, and directing him to leave mine in my room and Haley's in hers. The bags are clearly marked."

Pippins disappeared and Ginger allowed the horror she felt to show. "Oh my goodness, Haley. My father knew about this!" Heat exploded on her cheeks as the severity of the situation blossomed.

Haley placed a steady hand of comfort on her shoulder. "Now, don't jump to conclusions. We don't know why he instructed the door to this room to be locked. It could be for innocent reasons and someone else with the knowledge took advantage."

"Yes, yes, you're right," Ginger said, exhaling.

"All we know about the deceased is that she was a young female, and was about five feet, seven inches tall," Haley said.

"And likely died on the thirty-first of December 1913," Ginger added, "wearing a Lucile evening gown."

Ginger tried to imagine the events that led to this poor woman's death. And in Ginger's very own home—it was too much to take in! Her knees quivered but she was loath to sit on the dusty camp bed. She paced a small circle instead.

"What do you want to do now?" Haley asked.

"I wouldn't mind a lie down," Ginger said, fighting a sudden wave of fatigue. The time change from Boston combined with this shocking news had exhausted her both physically and emotionally.

Haley closed the door behind them, and Ginger locked it, depositing the key into her skirt pocket. They descended to the second floor.

"It looks like you're in this one," Ginger said, as the reached the first room where the door was sitting open.

"How do you know?"

Ginger glanced down the passage at the second bedroom door left open. "Because I always stay in that room. It was mine as a child. Besides, your suitcases are in

—
14

here."

"So they are," Haley said. Worry filled her dark eyes when she looked at Ginger. "Everything's going to be okay."

Ginger swallowed. "I hope so."

CHAPTER THREE

GINGER STILLED IN THE DOORWAY of her bedroom as a flood of memories washed over her. All of her childhood belongings had been long since packed away, and the large room was now a mature luxurious design with gold and ivory furnishings and trim. A full-length ornately trimmed mirror stood in the corner near a matching dressing table. Two striped ivory and gold chairs sat in front of the long windows, perfect for catching the daylight over tea and for journal writing. The bed featured prominently against one wall with an extravagantly carved wood head and footboard.

She'd shared that bed with Daniel. They played Frank Croxton on the gramophone and danced on the shiny wooden floor to *Road to Mandalay*.

Ginger sank into one of the chairs. Boss, always attuned to Ginger's emotions, climbed on her lap and nudged her cheek with his damp nose.

"Oh, Bossy. What would I do without you?"

Her fingers petted the animal as she stared blankly at her trunks, suitcases, and stacks of hatboxes.

The last time she'd seen her husband alive had been in the summer of 1918 in France. He thought she was there in her role as a telephone switchboard operator, and she'd let him believe that. Her real role in the war had allowed her to pull strings so they'd have a day and a night's leave together in a quaint little village near Marseille. For the twenty-four hours they were together, they agreed not to talk about the war. Ginger knew about the danger Daniel was in, and that he'd be heading back to Belgium the next day.

He had no idea how dangerous things were for her. He died before she could tell him the truth. It pained her that she had been denied the opportunity to explain.

A light tapping at the door snapped her to her senses.

"Come in," she called.

A young maid with dark hair pinned back and a friendly face stepped softly into the room, tea tray in hand, and curtsied. "Hello, Lady Gold. Mr. Pippins thought you'd like tea brought up."

"Yes, he's right. I would love a cup."

Lizzie poured. "Milk and sugar, madam?"

"Just milk. And what is your name?"

"Lizzie, madam." She bobbed again. "Mr. Pippins also suggested you might like help unpacking?"

"That would be fabulous. My Boston gal refused to accompany me," Ginger said. "Afraid of the water."

"Oh, that is sad, madam," Lizzie said. "To have such a grand opportunity and be stopped by a greater fear."

Ginger considered her new maid's perceptiveness.

Lizzie blushed, "Sorry, madam, I spoke out of turn."

"It's quite all right, Lizzie. You spoke the truth."

"I'll just be a minute to see if Miss Higgins would like tea, and I'll be right back."

Ginger smiled. "Of course." She knew Haley would turn her nose up at tea, being the devoted coffee drinker that she was, and wasn't a bit surprised when Lizzie returned almost immediately afterwards.

"Lizzie," Ginger said, brightening. "Let's start with the trunks, shall we?"

Unlike Haley, who'd helped on the steamship, Lizzie was well-versed in the different styles of dresses. "I was a lady's maid in my last job," she explained, "before she moved to Africa." Her face showed genuine appreciation for the quality of Ginger's evening gowns made of imported satiny-smooth silk, textured crepe, sheer chiffon and luscious velvet. "Are these from America?"

Ginger nodded at the obvious.

"They're so lovely!"

"Thank you, Lizzie. There are plenty of dress shops in Boston and New York. Are you familiar with the dress shops in London?" Ginger thought she might be able to track down the Lucile dress. Maybe she could find someone who knew something of the victim.

"Somewhat, madam. My previous lady often spoke of

them."

"I'd be delighted if you could come up with a list of the most popular shops."

"I suspect you'd want the salons?"

Ginger was pleased that this young girl seemed to know the difference. Salons designed and created unique dresses for each customer. Other shops had begun supplying more affordable factory-made dresses, a growing industry since the war especially with the younger flapper crowd. Ginger frequented both kinds.

Once Lizzie had emptied the trunks, she moved to the suitcases and hung the day dresses and tea dresses found there. Ginger busied herself by organizing her hats and accessories and putting away her jewellery and hatpins.

She remembered the photograph of her husband, so dashing in his lieutenant uniform, and removed it from her handbag.

Sir Daniel Livingston Gold, baronet, the one true love of her life. Ginger remembered how excited she had been to bring him here, to share her London home, and recount all her precious memories. Introducing her new husband to Pippins had been such a thrill. Ginger had thought Pippins to be tall, but her Daniel towered over him. With genuine warmth in his brown eyes and a sincere smile on his handsome face, he greeted Pippins with enthusiasm.

"Lady Gold speaks so highly of you, Mr. Pippins."

Pippins' eyes sparkled at her new title, his mouth pulling against his will into a grin. "You have a very fine bride, sir."

"I do, indeed!"

Ginger smiled at the memory. "Lizzie, is there a frame around I could use?" She held up the photo for size. "I only have this plastic travel frame. So much lighter, you see."

"Yes, madam. Is that Sir Daniel Gold, madam?"

"It is."

"He was very handsome," Lizzie bobbed quickly, "if you don't mind me saying so."

"I don't mind, and I agree."

Lizzie disappeared for a few moments and returned with an empty silver frame. Ginger slid the photo in behind the glass and set it on the night table beside her bed.

"It's perfect."

CHAPTER FOUR

A NAP DID LITTLE to alleviate the growing anxiety Ginger felt, but it did restore colour to her pallid complexion.

"I thought you would be ready for refreshments by now," Pippins said, when Ginger entered the sitting room. "And had them prepared."

Ginger was grateful for Pippins, not only for his efficiency at his role as butler but also to have a friendly and familiar face to help her resettle. Her father had loaned the butler out to a spinster cousin once the Great War had started, and Pippins had been with her this whole time. Old Cousin Enid had recently passed away, quietly in her sleep, releasing Pippins to serve once more at Hartigan House.

Ginger and Haley each claimed a wingback chair that curled around a large stone fireplace, and Boss settled on Ginger's lap. Lizzie poured the tea. Ginger caught her gaze lingering on Boss.

"Do you like dogs, Lizzie?"

"Oh yes, madam. I used to have a pet, but I had to leave him when I went into service. I do miss the old hound."

"I'll be needing help with Boss from time to time. You won't mind if I ask for your assistance?"

"Not at all, madam! I'd be pleased as punch!" She bobbed excitedly and left the room.

"The boss has a new friend already," Haley said wryly.

"He's the friendly type."

Lizzie arrived with salmon sandwiches, newly created, Ginger presumed, by the cook whom Ginger had yet to meet. When Ginger reassured the young maid that they lacked nothing, she and Haley were left alone.

Ginger sipped her tea and studied her surroundings. "Strong Victorian style," Ginger said.

"Oh?" Haley said. She wrinkled her nose at her tea, but sipped anyway.

"Yes, overly opulent and too many accessories and pieces of furniture. You can barely walk through here without bruising a hip." Ginger found the overcrowded room with its dark décor oppressive.

Haley nodded. "There's no shortage of places to sit."

Ginger agreed. "If you don't mind worn fabric and lumpy cushions. This house hasn't been updated since the turn of the century. I think that's what I'll do while I'm here. I'll renovate Hartigan House. New furniture, new floors. Clear the walls."

"That's ambitious," Haley said. "I thought you were planning to sell?"

In truth, Ginger didn't know what she should do. Boston *had* been home for twenty years, the city was in her blood; but London was her birthplace and her heritage. Her parents and her husband were buried nearby.

"Well, I can't very well sell it looking like this, can I? And a fresh look is sure to bring a higher selling price."

"I suppose you're right."

"And it's something for me to do while I'm waiting," Ginger said. "Otherwise I'll just be wandering this big house like a daft bat while you're improving your mind and giving practical aid to the citizens of London."

They'd had this conversation before. Fortunately Ginger had attended college before marriage—her studies in maths and languages were a huge asset during the war— but now, as a war widow, Ginger's only prospects were to remarry—something she was not ready to do.

George Hartigan had been an intuitive businessman leaving Ginger half of his business assets and this old house. The other half, along with the Boston house, was left to Ginger's American stepmother and half-sister. In that respect, she really didn't have a home there anymore.

"You're certainly not *daft*," Haley said, emphasizing Ginger's fall into British parlance. "I doubt you'll be wandering around for long. And don't forget..." She pointed upwards at the ceiling.

—

Ginger's fingers flew to her lips. "How could I forget that, even for a moment? It must be the time lag between Boston and London turning my brain to pea soup. How irreverent to discuss redecorating plans!"

"I'm certain the lady in red has no opinion at all," Haley said. "Besides, the police will handle everything and you'll have plenty of time to consider new colours and whatever else is involved in bringing about a change of interiors."

Pippins knocked on the door, and Ginger called him in.

"Lady Gold," he said, "I thought you'd like to be introduced to the housekeeper."

A sturdy, ruddy-faced woman with a cook's cap and well-used apron stepped forward.

"This is Mrs. Thornton. She is also the cook. You might remember her from your last visit in 1913."

Ginger did remember Mrs. Thornton from when she and her late husband Daniel passed through, though there hadn't been time to engage her much in conversation. She'd been the cook's assistant in those days and known as Miss Thornton. Apparently she'd been given the courtesy title of *Mrs.* Thornton in the meantime. She looked the same, stout with short, wiry hair under her cap. Her full cheeks tinged pink as she entered a slight curtsy.

"Hello again, Mrs. Thornton," Ginger said. "So marvellous that you could return to Hartigan House after so many years away."

"It's a pleasure to be back, madam," she said. "'Artigan 'Ouse is a wonderful place."

"Mrs. Thornton has prepared lamb stew and dumplings for dinner," Pippins said, "for whenever you are ready."

"That is so good of you, Mrs. Thornton," Ginger said, "I hadn't realised until now that I'm starving."

"Yes, thank you," Haley added.

"Pippins," Ginger called as he and Mrs. Thornton were leaving. The butler stepped back into the sitting room.

"Lady Gold?"

"Is that all the staff there are?" Ginger asked. "Just the three of you?"

"Madam, I took the liberty of hiring a cleaning company to help with opening up the house. I just recently brought on Lizzie Weaver so you and Miss Higgins could be attended to properly, but thought it best to wait for further instruction before employing more staff."

"Of course, Pippins."

The dining room had the same extravagant design as the sitting room. The springs in the seats were loose, poking one in a most uncomfortable and delicate manner, and the golden silk fabric worn thin in some places. Ginger noted the chips in some of the porcelain dishes.

"Hartigan House is in need of a bit of tender loving care," Ginger said to Haley when Mrs. Thornton and Pippins had left. "Less clutter, modern colours. New art. Yes, definitely new art for the walls." Ginger sighed. "If only there weren't a skeleton in the attic to cast a shadow over the whole affair."

Haley lifted a spoonful of stew. "Such an

inconvenience when one desires to redecorate."

"Isn't it, now. I suppose it was too much to ask to come to London, sign a few papers and sail back to Boston without having a crime to solve first." Especially one that might involve her father.

"It's not up to you to solve the crime, you know. Call the police."

"Haley, dear, you're newly exposed to high society, so you aren't aware how ravenous the wolves are. Socialites live for the next scandalous moment. It's their form of entertainment. Once news gets out that a corpse has been lying in Hartigan House for over a decade, it'll make the front-page news. It's not exactly how I wanted to get my photograph in the rags. We'll be the talk of the town; it'll be impossible to go out without encountering heated glares and indiscreet whispering." Ginger groaned. "And Lord help us if word gets out about my father's alleged telegram with instructions to keep the door locked."

"I understand," Haley said. "What if we kept the bit about the telegram to ourselves for now? We'll agree to release that piece of information if it becomes necessary to solving the case."

Ginger relented. "That won't keep the hounds away, but it's not like I haven't had to deal with unwanted attention before."

Lizzie scampered in when Ginger rang the bell. "Please ask Pippins to join us."

Moments later Pippins entered the room. He stood near the table, back straight and hands cupped against his abdomen.

—

"How can I be of service, Lady Gold?"

"First, please ensure that Lizzie and Mrs. Thornton are occupied elsewhere."

"Certainly, madam."

Pippins left the room.

"What are you doing?" Haley asked.

"I want to talk to Pips without interruption."

Pippins returned, giving Ginger his full attention.

"Mrs. Thornton is gathering marrow from the vegetable plot and Lizzie has taken, er, Boss, for a walk."

"Good. Pips, Miss Higgins and I believe it's time to call the police."

Haley shot Ginger a look of surprise.

"I see," Pippins said.

"But first, can I have your assurances to refrain from mentioning my father and the telegram? At least initially?"

"Of course."

"Terrific. Next, I'm assuming there are records kept of every gathering and soirée hosted at Hartigan House?"

"Yes, madam. Food, design, and entertainment were planned ahead of each event and meticulous accounts kept."

"Can you look back to the winter of 1913? Especially an event that would require evening attire?"

"I believe all the records were packed away and stored in Mr. Hartigan's, forgive me, I mean your study. Would you like me to search?"

"Yes, please."

Pippins bowed and left the room.

Haley's dark brows arched in question. "I thought

you wanted to wait a day to call the police?"

"It was just the shock of the moment. I needed time to sort it out, but I feel if we wait, it could be counted as a mark against us—should the investigation go wrong." Should her father be implicated, Ginger thought, but shame kept her from saying it aloud.

Haley inclined her head and stared at Ginger with soft eyes. "I'm sorry to be leaving you here alone."

"What do you mean?"

"I start my classes on Monday. I'm to move into the dormitory this weekend."

"Well, yes, I guess I knew you'd be going." Ginger poured on her native English charm and forced a smile. "Somehow I'll manage without you, old girl."

Pippins returned and stood near the wall until Ginger called him over.

"What did you find out?" she asked.

He opened an old ledger-style book. "Your father hosted a small New Year's soirée on the thirty-first of December 1913."

"How many people were in attendance?"

"A dozen, madam."

"I don't suppose there is a guest list?"

"There is, madam," Pippins said as he handed the ledger to Ginger. "It's recorded here."

Ginger laid the book on the table and scoured the page.

"Anyone you know?" Haley said.

Scanning the names, Ginger shook her head. "I grew up in Boston and didn't become familiar with my father's

London circle." She paused and then pointed. "Wait a minute, I know this one. Harriet McCallum."

"Oh?" Haley said.

"I remember her coming to visit us in Boston when I was younger. I do remember my stepmother being less than hospitable. "

"Sally?" Haley said facetiously. "I can't imagine."

"Oh yes. There was a moment when my father left the room that I thought Sally and Harriet McCallum were going to gouge each other's eyes out."

Haley smacked her thigh. "Oh, to be a fly on the wall."

"Miss McCallum had dark strawberry-blonde hair. I think she reminded Sally of my mother."

"Madam," Pippins said. "I do recall that Miss McCallum cancelled at the last minute. I forgot to cross out her name."

CHAPTER FIVE

ONE OF THE INSTRUCTIONS Ginger had forwarded to Pippins in regards to opening Hartigan House was to acquire a telephone.

"Please ring the police, Pippins."

Lizzie arrived to clean the dining table, and Ginger and Haley returned to the sitting room. "Oh, you're back," Ginger said. "Please, bring Boss to me when you're finished here."

Lizzie bobbed a curtsey. "Yes, madam."

The fire in the stone fireplace had cooled to embers. Haley added a log and stoked the coal until it ignited.

"The staff really ought to do that," Ginger said.

"I don't mind," Haley replied. "Besides, poor Lizzie is being run off her feet. She's dusting and vacuuming, making the beds, serving tea, helping Mrs. Thornton in the kitchen, *and* walking your dog."

"You're right. I need to hire someone to help her."

Boss bounded into the room with Lizzie after him.

"He's such a good dog, madam," Lizzie said. "So clever."

Ginger laughed and scrubbed her pet behind the ears. "Well, *he* certainly thinks so."

"How old is he, madam, if you don't mind me asking."

"He's five." Ginger recalled the moment her father had given the Boston terrier to her as a gift, shortly after she'd returned from France without Daniel. She had wetted the puppy with her tears for many weeks.

"Five? He acts like a pup!"

Lizzie bobbed and left them alone.

"Nice gal," Haley said.

"Yes. I quite like her."

Before too long the door chime rang and Pippins announced the police.

"Chief Inspector Reed and Sergeant Scott, madam."

Ginger rose to greet the inspector. She'd both been hoping he'd be assigned the case and dreading it. He wore a long jacket over a late summer linen suit and held a brown felt fedora in his hand. His dark hair was cut short around the ears—no sideburns—and slicked back with hair tonic, a hint of grey at his temples. His face was clean-shaven and pleasant to look upon.

"Inspector Reed, so good to see you again."

Basil Reed had been on the same steamship as

Ginger and Haley on their trip from Boston to Liverpool and they had only said their goodbyes the day before. The lines fanning from his eyes deepened as he smiled. "And you, Mrs. Gold, and so soon! Crime must follow you around."

"It's certainly not something I plan for," she said. "You remember Miss Higgins."

"Of course, your American friend." Basil Reed tipped his fedora to Haley, then added, "As introduced by your fine butler, this is Sergeant Scott."

Sergeant Scott removed his police hat and nodded. He was an older man with thinning hair, older than the inspector by a good decade. He wore a black police uniform buttoned down the middle and held a Brownie box camera in one hand. Unlike in Boston, the police in England didn't carry arms. Ginger shivered. A frightful thought.

Inspector Reed returned his attention to Ginger. "I'm told there's a body in the house?"

"Yes, unfortunately, this is true. This way, please."

Ginger led Inspector Reed and Sergeant Scott through to the servant's area and up the back staircase. Haley and Pippins followed behind with little Boss scampering along.

"I only just arrived today," Ginger said. "The house has been shut up for ten years and only just recently reopened."

"Why was it shut up for so long?"

"My father knew he'd be away for some time and then with the war and his illness, it was left empty for much longer than he'd first anticipated."

"Are you still going to sell?" he asked. Ginger had confided in the inspector about her indecision while on the SS *Rosa*. She glanced at Pippins whose facial expression showed no emotion.

"Nothing has been decided," Ginger said with a wave of her hand. "This is the sleeping quarters for the staff," Ginger explained as they entered the attic. "This area is the men's quarters. The body was found in the room at the very end." Ginger had gotten the skeleton key from Pips, which she now removed from a pocket of her embroidered jade-green crepe dress and unlocked the door. She allowed the inspector and constable to enter first.

"Not a recent crime," Sergeant Scott said, grimacing at the skeletal remains on the floor.

"Who made the discovery?" Basil Reed asked.

Ginger answered, "Mr. Pippins."

The inspector turned to Pippins. "When?"

"Yesterday, sir."

"And you didn't think to call us then?"

"Lady Gold was due to arrive shortly. I thought it best to await her instruction."

Basil Reed's eyebrows shot up as he stared back at Ginger. "*Lady* Gold?"

"You're not the only one with a surprise title." The inspector had introduced himself to Ginger as Mr. Basil Reed and only revealed his vocational title once he learnt a body had been found on board the ship.

"And pray tell, how does one become a Lady whilst residing in America?"

"My husband was a baronet. Sir Daniel Livingston Gold. Also a lieutenant in the British army."

"I see. I shall correct the way I address you in the future."

Ginger inclined her head. "I thought we had agreed on using our Christian names, Basil?"

"Ginger?"

Ginger was pleased that Basil had remembered. Ginger had been named after her father, George, but her mother had christened her Ginger because of Ginger's red hair.

Haley cleared her throat. "*Lady* Gold and Inspector Reed, what do you think about the dead body before us?"

Ginger had the decency to blush. Had she really entered a flirtatious banter with the inspector at a time like this?

Sergeant Scott gave Basil a sideways questioning glance before returning his attention to the Brownie pressed against his protruding stomach and continued to snap pictures.

Basil cleared his throat and focused on the remains. "Any idea who she is?"

"No," Ginger answered. "We believe she's been here for a decade, since the house was closed up."

"Why do you believe that?" Basil asked. "If the house was empty, someone could've broken in and committed the crime here. The perpetrator would have good reason to believe the body wouldn't be found for some time."

"Pippins," Ginger said, "were there any signs of a break-in when you first returned to Hartigan House?"

"No, madam. All the doors and windows were locked and untampered with."

"What about this window?" the inspector asked.

"I opened it, sir," Pippins said. "It was... stuffy."

"The decomposition is quite thorough," Haley said, bringing the conversation back to the time of death speculation. "Except for the stains on the floor, all the organs have dissolved, or, possibly, been eaten by rodents."

"And her dress is a Lucile, circa 1913," Ginger said.

Basil Reed looked impressed. "I take it 'Lucile' is a fashion term?"

"Lady Lucy Duff-Gordon designed under her formal name, Lucile."

Now that Ginger viewed the crime scene for the second time, without the initial shock, she could examine the situation with logic. If one could go by the quality of her clothing, she was from the upper classes. Quite possibly a guest of her father's.

"Any idea how the victim came to be in your house?" the inspector asked, "now that we've eliminated the break-in theory?"

"Pippins has kept good records of all the events hosted here," Ginger answered. "My father hosted a soirée in late December of that year. We have a guest list."

"I'd like to see that list," Inspector Reed said.

"Of course."

Basil Reed made notes in a small notebook he'd removed from his suit pocket. "Is the room exactly how you found it?"

"Yes, except for this." Ginger pointed to the small

bone she'd placed on the floor by the body. "Boss discovered the phalange under the bed."

"Quite honestly, I'm surprised more bones aren't scattered around the room," Basil said.

"The house is quite well built, sir," Pippins pointed out. "We've never had a rat problem at Hartigan House."

"You know, I never checked the drawers," Ginger said, moving quickly to the dresser before either Basil or the sergeant could stop her.

"Allow Sergeant Scott to do it," Basil said.

Ginger had the top drawer opened and her finger groping the inside. "I'm already here. Nothing in this one." She moved on to the next two. "All empty so far," she said.

She shifted her dress, squatted to access the last drawer, and almost announced the same verdict of empty when her fingers brushed against something in the back. Ensuring her body was blocking the inspector's view, she pocketed the item.

"Anything?" Basil Reed asked.

"Not so far." Ginger straightened her dress as she stood and motioned to the corpse. "We need to know who she is. I assume you have a record of missing persons from that year?"

"Yes." He turned to his sergeant. "Scott, get on that, will you? I want to know about every unsolved missing person's case from 1913 to present."

"Shall I go now, sir, or wait?"

"You can go now."

"How will you get back to the station?"

"I can walk or take a taxicab."

—

"I can drive you," Ginger said. "Pippins, father's motorcar is still in the garage, is it not?"

"Yes, madam."

"And running?"

"Yes, madam. It's been tuned up and filled with petrol, in anticipation of your arrival."

Ginger clapped her hands. "There, that settles it."

The sergeant left, and Basil continued his examination of the room, troubling himself to check the drawers for himself and coming away empty. "Whoever our killer was, knew about this room and that it was unoccupied."

Ginger didn't like the sound of that. It implied the murderer was someone *close*.

Who was this poor woman? Had her disappearance been reported?

"Miss Higgins," Inspector Reed said. "Do you have any medical observations you'd like to add?"

"Until the remains are laid out in a pathology lab, it's hard to say anything for sure."

"If I can use your telephone," Inspector Reed said. "I'll ring for the police to deliver the remains to the morgue."

"Certainly," Ginger said. "Pippins, show Inspector Reed the telephone."

The inspector followed the butler down the stairs, leaving Ginger and Haley alone. Ginger removed the notebook from her pocket.

Haley frowned. "What's that?"

"It was in the bottom drawer."

—

37

"That's what the police call evidence."

"I know. And I plan to hand it in. I just wanted a chance to look through it first."

Haley conceded. Had Ginger produced the small book when she'd discovered it, Inspector Reed would've confiscated it. "Well, open it up!"

"It's dated 1913. Andrew Bailey. I remember him. He was my father's valet. Mid-fifties, receding hairline. The nervous type." Ginger flipped through the pages with Haley looking on.

"Looks like Bailey kept notes on how to do his job," Ginger said. "Mr. H likes stiff collars. Mr. H wants his suits hung in a precise order, darks to lights. Mr. H doesn't like the grey bow tie. Keep the cabinet with Mr. H's cufflinks and tie clips locked."

Ginger hummed. "I wonder if things had started to go missing."

"Could be why he wanted his cabinet locked. Or perhaps that was merely protocol, and Bailey had forgotten to lock it."

Ginger continued to flip the pages. More instruction for Mr. Bailey and his duties.

"You have to give the guy credit," Haley said. "He wanted to do a good job."

"Wait, what is this?" On the next page, Ginger pointed to a line that was different from the others, not task-related at all.

Eunice came around again with Lord T. I don't trust her.

Ginger and Haley shared a look before glancing over at the remains.

—

"Do you think that's Eunice?" Ginger said.

"It's possible."

Ginger slipped the diary into her pocket and headed down the passage. Haley closed the door behind her. They met Pippins on the landing.

"Inspector Reed has finished with his telephone call, madam."

"Tell him I'll be right with him. I just need to freshen up."

Haley followed Pippins down, and Ginger returned to her room. Once inside she ran a comb through her red bob, reinforced the curls that rested on her jawline with her finger, and powdered her nose. She applied fresh lipstick and added a black hat with green lace trim, then collected a matching handbag.

She paused before the photo of Lieutenant Gold.

"I know I shouldn't be doing this, love. I promise I'll give it to the inspector soon." Ginger opened the small drawer in her night table and slipped Andrew Bailey's diary inside.

CHAPTER SIX

BASIL REED waited for Ginger in the sitting room, his neck craned as he studied the paintings on the wall.

"Someone is a fan of Waterhouse."

"My father. He loved *The Mermaid,* which is why it has prominence above the fireplace."

Basil's mouth twitched as he studied the image of a long-haired beauty, nude to the waist, her creamy arm positioned in such a way as to preserve the mythical creature's modesty. "It's very evocative."

"He told me once that she reminded him of my mother, especially the long red hair." Ginger laughed. "I do believe that's why my stepmother refused to allow him to bring it along to Boston."

Basil stared at her as if for the first time, causing

Ginger to glance away. Her hand went to the exposed skin at the base of her neck. "She's quite like you too, I imagine," he said.

Ginger giggled nervously and changed the subject. "Father appreciated all the classic painters, and liked to dabble in the craft on occasion. He said it helped him to relax and claimed he got his best business ideas while lost in his artwork."

"Was he any good?"

Ginger tilted her head up, pushing back the initial awkwardness, and caught his eye. "At art, no. But he was a superb businessman, made his fortune in American steel."

Basil cleared his throat and straightened his tie, and his voice took on its official business tone. "When was the last time Mr. Hartigan lived in Hartigan House?"

"1908, but he often returned for business."

Pippins approached. "The police are at the back door, madam."

"The back door?" She smiled at Basil. "Good thinking, Inspector. I don't know my neighbours, but I'm sure a police visit is enough to get the gossip mill going."

"Show them to the attic, Mr. Pippins," the inspector said.

"Should we go with them?" Ginger asked. "To make sure they don't damage the bones."

"They're professionals," Basil Reed said. "But, perhaps you're right."

Ginger and Basil Reed followed Pippins and the police to the crime scene.

With gloved hands the officers carefully lifted the

remains, including the red dress and underthings along with a good amount of dust, into a large metal pail. Ginger and Basil followed them down again and Ginger allowed that the work was done professionally.

"Are you still interested in driving me back to the Yard, Mrs..." He paused and corrected himself, "Lady Gold? I don't mind calling a taxicab."

"Oh, for goodness sake, do call me Ginger. The title thing... I'm not used to it. And yes, I'll drive you. The fastest way to the garage is through the kitchen."

Ginger led Basil Reed down the hall and through the green baize-servants' door. "I loved this passage as a child. Mrs. Smith was our cook back then, ran the kitchen with an iron fist. All bark and no bite, though. I'd often sneak in for freshly made biscuits and cake."

"I can imagine you were quite a precocious child."

"Oh, Inspector," Ginger said with a teasing lilt to her voice. "Why ever would you presume that?"

Mrs. Thornton stirred something in a large bowl using a long wooden spoon. She looked up, horrified at their unexpected arrival.

"So sorry to intrude, Mrs. Thornton," Ginger said. "We're just taking a shortcut to the garage."

Mrs. Thornton lowered her head and mumbled something Ginger couldn't quite discern.

Suddenly Boss trampled through with Lizzie calling after him, "Boss, Boss!"

Forgetting herself, Mrs. Thornton shouted back, "I told you to keep that dog out of the kitchen!" Then remembering Ginger there, "Excuse me, madam. Only I don't think it's sanitary."

"Of course, Mrs. Thornton, you're right. We'll take him with us."

"We will?" Basil Reed said. He stepped back and studied Boss with apprehension.

"That's right, I remember now from the ship. You're afraid of dogs."

"I'm not afraid. I just don't get on with them."

Ginger laughed. "All right then. Lizzie, do you mind keeping Boss for a while longer?"

Ginger tugged on the skirt of her dress and squatted low. She petted the small dog then lifted him to kiss him on the head. "You be a good boy," she said. Then to Lizzie, "Do keep him on a leash."

"Yes, madam."

Basil Reed motioned to the outside door, "This way?"

Ginger nodded and Basil held the door allowing her to exit first.

It was a short walk through the garden to the double motorcar garage. Built with the same stones as the house, the garage had wooden barn doors facing the alley. Further afield was the stable, long since empty, with tall weeds pressing against the stone walls and a mass of green vines reaching for the roof. Ginger missed having horses. Perhaps if she stayed…

"Pippins said he unlocked the doors," Ginger said.

Basil Reed opened the garage doors and the daylight hit the polished vehicle inside. Basil whistled. "A 1913 Daimler TE 30 Cranmore Landaulet."

"You know your automobiles."

"It's a hobby of mine."

"It's ten years old, but rarely driven. Father bought it so Daniel and I would have something to drive when we came on our honeymoon."

"A beaut."

Ginger almost strutted to the left side of the motorcar before remembering she was in England and made a quick adjustment to her step, which took her to the right side where the steering wheel was.

"Would you like me to drive?" Basil Reed asked.

"I know how to drive," Ginger returned.

"I've no doubt, but how long has it been since you've driven on the left side of the road."

"I drove this very motorcar the last time I was here."

"Ten years ago!"

Ginger grimaced. She knew how to drive. She drove almost daily in Boston—though there she owned a '22 cherry-red Sainte Claire Roadster—and often in France during the war she had found herself behind the wheel. Both were places where driving happened on the right-hand side. The last time she had driven on the left was over ten years ago, and there was far less traffic to deal with then. She wanted to show Basil Reed she was a capable and competent woman, but getting in a car accident because of her pride most certainly wouldn't give her that.

"All right, Inspector," she said reluctantly. "You can drive."

Basil Reed hesitated. "Then how will you get back? I think I'll wave down a taxicab."

Ginger's shoulder's slumped. She wanted to see Scotland Yard, but the inspector had a point. She stepped away from the motorcar.

"Okay, well, it was good seeing you again, Inspector, even if the circumstances were unsavoury."

"Indeed." The inspector tipped his hat. "Good evening, Lady Gold."

Basil Reed walked steadily along the flat-stone pathway that led around the house to the front gate. Ginger called out, "You'll let me know if you uncover anything, won't you?"

The inspector paused and called back over his shoulder. "Leave this to the police, madam."

Ginger made a face and strolled back to the house. She didn't fail to notice how they'd gone back to formal names.

CHAPTER SEVEN

GINGER AROSE EARLY the next morning to practice driving the Daimler. Pippins gave her a look of fatherly-type concern.

"Do be careful, madam. There's more traffic on the roads now. Are you sure you don't want me to take you out?"

"I need to do this myself, Pips, but thank you for offering."

Mrs. Thornton looked downright frightened. She muttered, "I'm just glad I'm safe here in the kitchen."

"I think it's so exciting for a woman to drive a motorcar just like a man," Lizzie said.

"It *is* exciting, Lizzie," Ginger said. "And once I'm comfortable driving here, I'll take you for a ride."

"That would be a spiffing, madam." Lizzie's eyes shone with wonder. "Thank you, madam."

Ginger adjusted her driving jacket and tugged on her leather gloves. "Come Boss. Let's have some fun!"

The Boston terrier followed his mistress outside, his stubby tail wagging. Ginger opened the two doors to the garage and stared at the flat-back carriage of the motorcar. She circled around the old two-door automobile. It was painted deep blue with a rich brown leather interior and had a black, flat carriage roof. The tire spokes were painted a pleasant contrasting yellow.

"I will not be intimidated by you," Ginger said under her breath. She made one erroneous step to the left of the motorcar before correcting herself. She opened the back door for Boss. "Get in."

Boss panted happily. He'd been on many motorcar rides in Boston. He sat by the window, which Ginger had lowered and stuck out his little black and white head.

The dashboard of the Daimler was much different from the Sainte Claire. Ginger focused on remembering the last time she'd driven it. It was a sunny summer day in August of 1913, and she'd surprised Daniel with a picnic. They sat on a bench in Kensington Gardens next to the round pond eating finger sandwiches that Mrs. Thornton had packed and feeding each other red grapes. Two elegant mute swans had swum close, and pressed their orange beaks together like lovers. Daniel had kissed her then.

"Set the ignition," Ginger said aloud. "set the throttle, set the choke." She searched the floor. "Push the starter button." She pressed the button with her left cap-toed Oxford shoe, and the engine puttered to life.

She pushed the clutch to the floor and put the motorcar into reverse, feeling somewhat unsteady using her left hand. Slowly releasing the clutch and adding petrol, she managed to reverse out of the garage without mishap.

The lane at the back of the house was only wide enough for one vehicle, and thankfully, Ginger was alone on the road. The gears ground as she searched for second and emitted a blast of smoke through the exhaust pipe.

"Come on, old girl," Ginger said as she gripped the steering wheel. Even though the lane was flat, Ginger was unused to seeing the ditch on her right side and overcompensated by nearly sideswiping a wild blackthorn tree on the left. Sweat had formed on her upper lip when she hit the main road.

Ginger pulled onto the two-way road, chanting to herself, "Stay left, stay left." She stuck to the residential area, and only had two close calls—one with a chap on a bicycle and the other with a dustbin lorry that made a right-hand turn in front of her.

At least Boss seemed to be having a good time, his head to the wind and barking at other dogs out walking with their owners.

By the time Ginger returned she felt exhausted but satisfied that she could drive properly in London without killing anyone. She pulled into the garage and turned off the engine. Looking back at Boss she said, "Wasn't that fun?"

Boss barked in response and shimmied with excitement. As Ginger reached back to pat his head her eyes caught sight of a strip of red fabric caught on the mechanism behind the passenger seat. She carefully released it and held it up to the light. A high quality satin.

Her stomach tightened at her next thought: the attic victim wore a red satin dress. Was it possible she had travelled in the Daimler? And if so, had her father been driving? Her shoulders drooped as she pinched her eyes together. Evidence was pointing toward her father's guilt. She should drop her involvement in this investigation and concern herself with preparing Hartigan House to sell. A large redecoration project was exactly what she needed to get her mind off this case.

The French windows of the morning room opened onto the garden veranda, and Ginger found Haley seated at the table and eating.

"Where were you?" Haley said before taking a bite of her croissant.

Ginger peeled off her gloves. "I needed to brush up my skills with the motorcar."

"You're braver than me," Haley said. "I don't think I could ever get used to driving on the wrong side of the road."

"It's not the *wrong* side of the road," Ginger said as she claimed a chair across from Haley. "It's the *other* side of the road."

Haley snorted. "Same thing as far as I'm concerned. By the way, where do I catch one of those buses? I have to check into the London School of Medicine for Women today."

"Wait a minute," Ginger paused holding her coffee

mug halfway to her mouth. "You're moving out today?"

"Yes. I told you didn't I?"

Ginger placed her coffee back onto the table without sipping. "Well, yes, you did. I just didn't realise it was time already."

"It's not like we won't see each other. We can visit on weekends."

"It's *at the weekend*, if you're going to fit in here, my American friend." Ginger smiled, but inwardly she felt loss seeping in. Must she lose everyone dear to her? Once Haley was established at the university, she'd be too busy with her studies and her new academically minded friends to want to spend time with a boring *Lady* with nothing better to do than shop and gossip.

Ginger jangled her motorcar keys in the air. "You must let me drive you."

"I would like to get there in one piece if you don't mind."

"Look here, I'm a great driver. I used to drive here, you know, on the *other* side of the road. It comes back like riding a bike."

"Well, it would be more convenient than me having to lug my suitcases on and off a bus."

"Exactly!"

Ginger decided to see things on the bright side. She had a motorcar and could meet up with Haley anytime. Besides, she wasn't even planning to stay in London. She was going to have to let go of the friendship eventually.

"I need to call in at Scotland Yard anyway, so I can do that after I drop you off."

Haley's dark eyebrows raised. "Scotland Yard, huh."

"Not to see Inspector Reed," Ginger answered quickly, recognizing the tease. "At least not specifically. I want to know if the guest list I gave him helped to identify the woman, that's all. Plus, I have evidence to drop off."

"You mean Andrew Bailey's notebook? Did you find anything new?"

"Sadly, not. Only that cryptic mention of a woman named Eunice."

Ginger removed a folded handkerchief from her pocket. "I found this in the Daimler." She opened the handkerchief on the table revealing the torn fabric.

"What is it?" Haley asked.

"A strip of satin."

Haley's dark eyes flashed with understanding. "Not from…"

"Oh, Haley, I hope not. Is there a way we can know for certain?"

"A forensic lab could do a comparison." She looked at Ginger compassionately. "Either way, I'm sure it's a coincidence. Your father could've lent his car to someone."

"Yes, that must be it." Ginger was relieved to have a reason to exclude her father from the equation. "Do you want to come to the Yard with me? I could drop you off at the university afterwards."

Haley checked her wristwatch, and her wide jaw broke into a smile. "I have time."

CHAPTER EIGHT

GINGER CHANGED out of her driving clothes while Haley packed up. The weather had cooled prompting Ginger to choose a blue wool suit with a narrow skirt that ended mid-calf. She spruced the look up with a white straw hat that had a low rim on one side and was decorated with a wide purple ribbon. She secured it to the left side of her bob with a pearl-tipped hatpin.

Before long, she and Haley were on their way rumbling through Green Park and adjacent to St. James's Park.

"No need to hold onto your hat," Ginger reprimanded. "I'm not going to smash into anyone."

Haley held the door firmly with one gloved hand and her felt cloche with the other. "I'm not sharing your certainty."

Ginger laughed aloud as they circled Trafalgar Square and motored down Whitehall. She looked over to Haley. "I'm quite enjoying this!"

"Keep your eyes on the road!"

Ginger pulled into the parking area at the back of Scotland Yard and the motorcar shuttered to a stop.

"Is it always supposed to do that?" Haley said, finally letting go of her hat.

"The poor thing hasn't been driven in years. It's just coughing up what's settled."

Haley opened her door. "Driving on the left makes *me* feel unsettled. I just might let out my own belch."

"Haley!"

"Don't worry. I won't do it in front of your inspector."

"He's not *my* inspector. Now, are you coming or not?"

Haley stepped up beside Ginger, and Ginger noticed that her friend did appear a bit pale. Perhaps on the trip to the university, she should slow down a little.

Situated on the Victoria Embankment along the Thames, New Scotland Yard comprised two four-storey Victorian-style buildings in banded red brick and white Portland stone.

Ginger approached the receptionist. "We're here to see Chief Inspector Reed."

The receptionist pushed her spectacles up along her narrow nose and squinted up at them. "Is he expecting you?"

"Yes," Ginger said without hesitation.

Knowing Ginger hadn't called ahead of time, Haley shot her a look.

"Tell him Miss Higgins and Lady Gold are here."

The receptionist straightened at the mention of Ginger's title.

"Yes, madam." She jumped up and brushed out her skirt. "Right away, madam."

"That's quite the secret weapon you have, *Lady* Gold," Haley said.

Ginger pursed her lips. "I figure I might as well use it while I'm here since it's no good to me in Boston."

The receptionist scurried back. "Right this way, Lady Gold, Miss Higgins."

The woman led Ginger and Haley to a large corner room down a narrow corridor. The windows faced south with a view of the Thames. The furniture was simple but smart, with a large wooden desk, shelving, and file cabinets. A felt fedora and an overcoat hung from a hat stand in the corner.

"I can't seem to go a day without an encounter with you two," the inspector said when they entered.

Ginger smirked. "Aren't you lucky?"

"I suppose I am." Basil returned to his chair and leaned back. "Now what can I do for you?"

"Were you able to identify the victim?" Ginger asked. She slid into the lone chair opposite the desk, while Haley hovered to her side.

Basil Reed threaded his hands together and leaned forward. "Unfortunately, we were unable to match up a

---

54

name from your guest list to one on our missing persons' register. I'm sorry to say, the victim is still unidentified."

"That's terrible!" Ginger said. "There must be something you can do to identify her?"

"Do not fear, Lady Gold. We're working on it."

Ginger huffed.

"She has more evidence to present," Haley said.

Ginger glanced at her with tight lips. She hadn't decided she was ready to relinquish the notebook. She started with the strip of satin. "I found this in the Daimler," she said as she opened the handkerchief. "The passenger side."

"Don't tell me you drove here."

"I did, and quite proficiently. Isn't that right, Haley?"

"Like a pro."

Basil Reed returned his attention to the piece of fabric in front of him. "Are you proposing it belonged to the victim?"

"A lab analysis might lend credence to the theory," Haley said.

"Yes," Basil Reed conceded. He stared at Ginger. "You're aware this would implicate your father."

"I'm sure he lent the motorcar to a friend."

"Right. Is there anything else?"

Ginger shook her head while Haley knocked her foot against Ginger's ankle.

"Ow."

"I'm sorry," Haley said. "I can be so clumsy. There is also a notebook."

Ginger snorted at Haley then smiled at the inspector.

—

"There was a notebook *behind* the dresser." She added with a straight face, "I took another look after you left." She removed it from her handbag and handed it to Inspector Reed. "It belonged to Andrew Bailey, a former valet of my father's."

Basil Reed stared at her with suspicion. "Sergeant Scott investigated the room thoroughly, including behind the dresser."

"The notebook is black and was difficult to see. I almost missed it too."

Basil inhaled then flipped through the small book. He glanced up at Ginger when he got to the end. "Who is Eunice?"

"I'm afraid I don't know."

The inspector opened a desk drawer and pulled out a sheet of paper. "This is the Yard's missing person list. Aha, I thought I saw it here." He turned the sheet and pointed. "Eunice Hathaway."

"Eunice isn't a common name," Ginger said, "but it's not unique either. It might not be the same person."

"We will investigate until we know for sure."

"You'll let me know?"

Basil Reed hesitated, then said, "Yes, Lady Gold. I'll ring you."

"Thank you, Inspector Reed."

They were undeniably back to English formality.

On the road, Ginger glanced at her worried-looking friend. "I think I'm getting the hang of driving on the left."

"Keep your eyes on the road!"

"My dear, you underestimate my skills."

Haley pressed her lips together and kept her gaze focused on the road as if by sheer will she could keep the Daimler in its lane.

"Oh, look," Ginger said, pointing to a grand Romanesque structure with six massive white pillars gracing the front balcony. "The Royal Opera House! We should go sometime."

"If we live through this, I'll acquiesce."

The drive was longer than Haley had imagined, not at all helped by traffic congestion. Horse and carriage traffic plodded alongside the motorcars, trams and double-decker buses. Pedestrians darted across busy streets while whistle-blowing traffic police kept order at the crossroads.

"Pippins was right when he said there was more traffic in the city now," Ginger said. "But we'll be at the medical school shortly."

They drove past Brunswick Square Gardens to the corner of Hunter Street and Handel Street.

"Soon-to-be-Doctor Higgins," Ginger said with a big smile. "You are here."

Haley grabbed her two suitcases from the back seat and she and Ginger approached the front door. The four-storey redbrick building breathed academia. Chiselled in jade-green stone above the arched doorway were the words: LONDON ROYAL FREE HOSPITAL SCHOOL OF MEDICINE FOR WOMEN.

"This is to be my home for the next two years," Haley said. "It's lovely."

Ginger ignored the hollow feeling she felt at the

thought of leaving Haley behind and opened the heavy wooden door, allowing Haley to enter first.

There was an air of purpose and importance about the place. The female students and staff alike walked quickly through the hallways, not stopping to chat or loiter about. This institution was a place for women who took their studies seriously.

"You'll fit right in," Ginger said.

Haley smiled. "I hope so. But they're all so young."

"You're young."

"I don't think those girls would consider thirty-two to be young," Haley said. "They'll think of me as an old spinster."

"No, they won't. They'll admire your maturity and intellect."

"You really should go into politics."

"I'm lucky I'm old enough to vote here," Ginger said referencing the thirty-years-of-age threshold British women had to cross before being given the vote. No such restriction was imposed on Ginger's American counterparts.

Haley approached the registrar, a thin middle-aged woman in a fitted wool suit, and gave her name.

"Miss Higgins, we're so happy to have you here. I'm Miss Knight. Please leave your bags here, behind the counter, and I'll show you around."

Haley dropped her bags off then made introductions. "This is my friend, Lady Gold."

Ginger glanced at her with annoyance, and Haley mouthed, "When in Rome…"

Miss Knight held out her hand. "Lady Gold, so nice to meet you!"

Miss Knight loved her job and showed Ginger and Haley the layout of the school like it was her first time doing so. "The labs are newly outfitted with all the latest equipment. I hear the forensic programme is very exciting." She presented the library, the lecture theatres, and the cafeteria. "Our cook is from France, and the food is *très délicieux.*"

Ginger grinned at Miss Knight's attempt at a French accent.

"Where are the dorms?" Haley asked. "I would like to get settled in."

For the first time the smile fell from Miss Knight's face and she nervously wrung her hands.

"Well, the thing is Miss Higgins, our school has become very popular and we give dorm priority to our first-year registrants. Since you are third year, well, many of our older students have taken flats in the city and commute here…"

Haley frowned. "Are you saying I don't have a room?"

"We had hoped we'd have a place for you, but it turns out … well, we might be able to squeeze in a camp bed with … we'd have to discuss it with the students themselves first. I truly am sorry. I meant to ring you this afternoon."

"That's quite all right, Miss Knight," Ginger said, "Miss Higgins can stay with me. I'd be happy to drive her."

Haley let out a small groan. "I can catch one of those

red General buses …"

Ignoring her friend's subtle protest, Ginger continued, "Perhaps I could even sit in on a lecture or two."

Miss Knight's smile returned to her face. "I'm sure that could be arranged, Lady Gold."

Haley gathered her suitcases. "Are you sure my staying with you is okay? That wasn't part of the arrangement."

"It's more than okay," Ginger said. "What are Boss and I going to do in that big house alone, anyway? Besides, you already have a room."

Miss Knight gave Haley her course schedule and an omnibus transit booklet. "There's also the underground railway," she said. "The Piccadilly line runs from South Kensington to Russell Square."

As they headed out, Haley muttered, "I won't be caught dead underground."

"Oh, silly, they're perfectly safe."

"I prefer the light of day."

"Don't tell me you suffer from claustrophobia?"

"There's no shame in it if I do."

Ginger honked at a wayward horse and cart as she rambled through Paddington, and Haley almost went blue from holding her breath.

Ginger was triumphant when she eventually eased the Daimler into the garage. "Now admit it," she said. "My driving skills on the way back were nearly perfect."

Haley mustered up a reply. "The drive through Hyde Park was particularly grand."

"I agree."

Pippins must've been watching for Ginger's arrival as he greeted them in the garden before they reached the morning room.

"What is it?" Ginger asked. "Is something wrong?"

"Nothing amiss, madam, only you have unexpected guests."

"I do? Who's here?"

"Lady Ambrosia Gold and Miss Felicia Gold, madam."

Ginger gripped Haley's arm. "*Oh mercy.* You're about to meet my in-laws."

CHAPTER NINE

"THERE YOU ARE!" The Dowager Lady Gold said when Ginger and Haley entered the sitting room. Ambrosia and her granddaughter Felicia occupied the wingback chairs angled in front of a well-stoked fire. Ambrosia sat upright, poised, ankles crossed, a silver-handled walking stick propped up beside her, while Felicia, a slight girl with grey eyes and sporting a wavy dark brown bob, curled up lazily. Her fashionable double-strap pump shoes were tossed to one side on the Turkish carpet. Lizzie poured everyone another cup of tea.

"Hello, Grandmother Gold, Felicia! Such a surprise!"

Ginger bent over to kiss the elderly woman on a soft, plump cheek.

Ambrosia replied, "Since we're family Georgia, I beg

your pardon me, *Ginger*, I thought we could drop in."

After much persuasion by Daniel, the Dowager Lady Gold had agreed to stop calling his wife Georgia, the formal first name found on Ginger's birth certificate. Ginger was named after her father, George Hartigan, but her mother had christened her Ginger due to her red hair.

"No telling how long it would take you to remember us and extend an invitation," Ambrosia continued.

"Oh, I could never forget you, Grandmother," Ginger replied.

Felicia stood to greet her sister in-law. She had a sweet heart-shaped face with bright eyes and rosebud lips. Her rich, brunette bob was set in perfect finger waves and shone under the electric lights. She wore an orange chiffon day dress that hung loosely on her slender frame, with a satin sash-belt low on the hips, sleeves slit from the shoulders to the wrist and a hemline only just below the knee. It was bold and brave and made Ginger smile. "Dear Felicia." Her voice was warm as she embraced her. "You've become such a beautiful young lady!"

"Thank you, Ginger. It's so, so good to see you again. I thought we'd never—"

"Of course we would," Ginger interjected. "And I'm here for an entire month."

Felicia's smile disappeared. "But, I thought you were moving here. To stay."

"I'm not sure what I'm doing, darling, but let's not worry about it today. Today we celebrate being together once again." She drew Haley into the circle.

"Grandmother and Felicia, this is my dear friend

Miss Higgins. She is lodging with me while a student at the London School of Medicine for Women. Haley, this is the Dowager Lady Gold and Miss Felicia Gold."

Haley extended her hand to each of them in turn. "How do you do?"

"You're American?" Ambrosia said with a hint of distrust in her voice.

"Yes, ma'am. From Boston."

"Madam. Ma'am is reserved for Queen Mary."

"Of course, madam," Haley said. "We use the term casually in America. It just slipped out."

Ambrosia sipped her tea then asked. "So, why are you in London, Miss Higgins?"

"I served in London as a nurse in the war. I fell in love with the city."

"Oh, I would so love to go to America one day," Felicia gushed. "Such an adventure!" Then she pouted. "I've never been anywhere."

Ambrosia shuffled in her seat, "Where is your footman? Our luggage is waiting in the foyer."

Ginger blinked. "Your luggage?"

"Yes, Ginger. We've come all the way from Hertfordshire. Surely, you recall how long a train ride one must endure getting here. We're staying over the weekend, at least. And I didn't bring my maid, since I thought for my short visit here, you wouldn't mind lending me yours."

Ginger kept her expression neutral but suddenly she felt exhausted. "I'm afraid we have a skeleton crew at the moment." She bit her lip at her poor choice of words. How awful it would've been had she made a slip of the tongue and said "skeleton in the attic."

"As you know, Hartigan House has been shut up for the last ten years," she continued quickly. "I haven't had a chance to do any hiring since I only arrived yesterday. The maid, Lizzie, can attend to you. I'm sure Pippins can take your luggage up."

Pippins, who'd been standing to the side, nodded at Ginger and left the room.

"I'll help," Haley said then followed him. "I have my own suitcases to take up, too."

Pippins and Haley disappeared leaving Ginger alone with her new guests.

"Skeleton crew," the Dowager Lady Gold muttered as she took another sip of tea.

Ginger showed her guests to their rooms. Ambrosia, being elderly, slept every afternoon, while Ginger and Haley, suffering the effects of the time difference between Boston and London, succumbed to the suggestion of a short, midday sleep. Only Felicia had the energy to make something of the afternoon and borrowed the Daimler to shop in the city.

The three nappers regrouped later that evening for dinner. Mrs. Thornton showed herself to be a wizard at producing a splendid three-course meal at short notice. Leek soup, steak and kidney pie and ending with apple crumble with custard.

Ginger and Haley sat opposite Ambrosia who appeared flustered at Felicia's absence. "She's a bit of a wild one," she said. "I did my best but I was too old to take on the duties of motherhood. When my son and his wife died in that crash, my heart broke of course, but taking care of little Felicia and young Daniel kept me too busy to linger in sorrow. I suppose that was a silver lining. Daniel was older and an old soul—as you well know, Ginger—and stepped right into the role of man of the house. God bless him. But Felicia... I even hired a nanny and a governess, but she ran rings around us all."

"I'm sure she's just lost track of time," Ginger said. "The city has a way of doing that. We can start without her." She passed the dishes around for each of them to fill their plates.

"How are things at Bray Manor?" Ginger asked.

Ambrosia put her fork down and sighed. "It's large and lonely."

"Oh, Grandmother," Ginger said. "Miss Higgins and I will come to visit you as soon as we can, isn't that right, Haley?"

Haley gave Ginger a sideways glance then replied, "I'd be happy to join Lady Gold if I can take time from my studies."

"The grounds are going to pieces, too," Ambrosia said. "We can't afford to employ enough staff."

Ginger blinked. She knew how much money came from the Hartigan estate to prop up the large property. Keeping Bray Manor running was part of her marital agreement. Father's contribution, now hers, should be more than enough, and Ginger wasn't prepared to invest more. "Perhaps I can have a look at the books when I come. See what we can do."

"Thank you, dear," Ambrosia said. "I hate to bother you with our family's troubles. As you know, my husband, Sir Artemis—God rest his soul—had a terrible gambling addiction. His sins have indeed been visited upon his children and children's children. We've been suffering from his losses ever since."

The back door of the house slammed. Felicia blew in with her arms full of packages and her face flushed with excitement. "First I went to Harrods—quite obviously, I need a new autumn-season wardrobe." She removed a fox fur shawl and wrapped in around her shoulders, the head of the animal over her chest and the tail down her back. She spun on her heels to display it.

"Isn't it fabulous?"

Ambrosia stared with mouth dropped open. "You're not going to wear a *dead* animal on your person!"

"Indeed I am, Grandmama. It's all the rage! What do you think, Ginger?"

"It's quite glamorous, darling."

Haley muttered, "In a morbid kind of way."

Felicia's good spirits would not be squashed. "After Harrods I went to the theatre district—so thrilling! I would go to a new show every night if I wasn't held captive in the country. Oh Ginger, darling, I'm afraid the old Daimler might be in need of petrol—the looks the old thing got! You really should get something new."

"Good heavens, child, take a breath!" Ambrosia said.

Felicia claimed the empty chair beside her grandmother. "Grandmama, we really need to move into the city. I shall simply die an old spinster at Bray Manor, shan't I, Ginger? The war has robbed Hertfordshire of all the young men. Ginger, you have loads of space here—might I not move in with you?"

Ambrosia dropped her fork. The clang of silver on porcelain reverberated along the high ceilings. For a moment, everyone forgot to breathe.

"Don't be a young fool," Ambrosia sputtered. "You can't just *invite* yourself to live with whomever you please."

"Oh, Grandmama. It's not like Ginger's a stranger. She's my *sister.*"

"Felicia," Ginger said calmly. "You are always welcome at Hartigan House, however, you can't possibly think of leaving your grandmother alone in the country?"

"I'm twenty-one years old! Am I expected to live at Bray Manor until she dies?"

"Felicia!" Ginger said, alarmed by her young sister's lack of propriety.

Felicia had the decency to cast a sheepish glance at Ambrosia who just tutted.

"But am I? I have no money of my own and no way to make any. There aren't any decent eligible bachelors in Hertfordshire to speak off. I'm going to grow old and die alone!"

"You must not get so worked up," Ginger said, "I'm certain …"

Felicia perked up and interrupted. "Grandmama can move here, too!"

"That is quite enough, young lady!" Ambrosia said. "I forbid you to go into town alone again—look at the nonsense you've picked up there!"

"Grandmama!" Felicia whined. "You can't be serious."

"I've never been more serious in my life," Ambrosia said firmly. To Ginger she added, "I do apologise. Felicia's always been a bit headstrong."

Felicia snorted.

"It's all moot anyway," Ginger said. "I plan to sell Hartigan House and go back to Boston."

Both Ambrosia and Felicia stared back at her with slack jaws.

"You're leaving us?" Felicia finally said.

Ginger's heart pinged at the note of loss in her young sister-in-law's voice.

"Well, eventually dear, I have to. My mother and sister…"

"Of course," Felicia said. She straightened, thrust her chin out. Something in her eyes flickered out. Hope?

Ginger felt horrid. Felicia had suffered so much loss in her short life. Belatedly Ginger understood that Felicia's desire to move in wasn't for the ease of shopping in town, but to be closer to her.

"Felicia, darling," she said kindly. "Nothing is settled yet. The truth is, I'm not certain what I'm going to do. The only thing I'm sure of is I need to redecorate, should I sell or should I stay. Would you like to help me with that?"

Felicia seemed to soften at the invitation. "I might as well be of some use since I'm here anyway."

"I hate to interrupt," Haley said, "but would you mind passing the butter?"

CHAPTER TEN

GINGER INTERCEPTED HALEY the next morning as she rushed down the steps.

"Where are you off to in such a hurry?"

Haley pushed stray curls from her dark eyes as she glanced over her shoulder. "I've got a bus to catch."

Ginger scurried to catch up, Boss on her heels, arriving with Haley at the door. "Are you going to the medical school? I can drive you?"

Haley smiled as she slipped into her tweed suit jacket and pressed her felt cloche more firmly on her head. "It's quite all right, Ginger. I think I'll enjoy the chance to take in the views." She slipped on her gloves and smirked. "Without having to worry if I'll live to see the next crossroad."

"Pfft. You were perfectly safe."

"Maybe so, but don't you have shopping to do with your sister-in-law today?"

"Quite right. Off you go then. Do pay attention—I want a full report when you get back."

Haley saluted. "Yes, madam."

Ginger closed the door behind her friend then called Boss to follow her to the kitchen.

"Lizzie, have you seen Miss Felicia?"

The maid dipped in a curtsey. "She's not been down for breakfast yet, madam."

"Oh dear," Ginger said. "I remember when I could sleep like that. I'll go and rouse her. Please ask Mrs. Thornton to warm something up for her. Come on, Boss."

A knock on Felicia's door produced a muffled groan. Ginger let herself in.

"Felicia, darling. If you're coming shopping with me, you must get up."

Ginger pulled the heavy curtains wide, and Felicia moaned. "Turn it off."

"I can't turn off the sun, love. You should be pleased that it's not raining. Let's enjoy this perfect day while we can." Ginger motioned to Boss to jump on the bed.

"Good boy, Boss," she said. Boss sniffed Felicia and rubbed a wet nose across her cheek.

"Ew, get off me you wretched beast!"

"Boss is not wretched, if you please, simply obedient to my commands. He's not going to stop molesting you until you get up."

"Fine." Felicia pulled herself into a sitting position. Her short hair was plastered messily to one side. Eyes

—

71

squinty and puffy, she held a hand up to shield them from the sunlight. "I'm coming."

"Good. Mrs. Thornton has your breakfast waiting. We really do have a lot to do, so make haste."

Ginger decided the time she spent waiting would do to take Boss for a walk. It'd been years since she'd strolled through the neighbourhood. Boss was excited about the venture, stopping every few minutes to mark his territory. Mallowan Court was an upper-class neighbourhood and Hartigan House nestled in loosely with other similarly grand homes. None had the elegance and sophistication they had had before the Great War lashed their nation. Soot from the industrial area had found them too. Windows needed cleaning, brickwork replacing, gardens trimming. The homes appeared tired, but with some of them, there were signs of renewal. Ginger waved to her neighbours as she passed and was waved to, but she didn't know any of them, and of course, they didn't know who she was.

She circled back in time to witness an older, well-dressed woman being led out of the house next door by a younger man. The woman called out when she saw Ginger.

"Are you Lady Gold?"

Ginger approached and signalled to Boss to sit on the pavement by her feet.

"I am." On closer inspection Ginger recognised the woman from her last visit. A decade had made her neighbour's hair go completely white. "Mrs. Schofield?"

Mrs. Schofield took Ginger's gloved hand with her own. "You remembered! My dear, my condolences on the loss of your father—and of your husband—I heard he didn't make it through the terrible fighting. So much loss for one so young."

"Thank you, Mrs. Schofield."

"Both wonderful men. I was blessed to know them."

"It's so gracious of you to say."

Mrs. Schofield motioned to the young man to step closer. "This is my grandson, Lieutenant Alfred Schofield." She added proudly, "He flew in the Royal Flying Corps in the war."

Lieutenant Schofield was handsomely dressed in a pinstriped, double-breasted suit. His facial features were boyish, but his stature and gait spoke of one who'd been enlisted. He doffed his straw hat. "Pleased to meet you Lady Gold." He motioned to Hartigan House. "Have you moved in?"

"Yes, well, no." Ginger laughed. "I'm not quite sure. I've just recently arrived from America to settle Father's estate here. I'm not sure if I should stay or sell."

Lieutenant Schofield looked at her with interest. "I should hope you will stay. I'm sure you'd add so much to London society."

London society wasn't much of an interest to Ginger, but she smiled and nodded anyway.

"Perhaps I can show you around sometime," Lieutenant Schofield said.

"Perhaps," Ginger said, "once I'm more settled. I really have so much to do."

"Of course." Lieutenant Schofield grinned slyly. "I know where you live."

Ginger wasn't quite sure how to take the comment.

With humour, she supposed and hoped that was how he intended it. She chuckled.

Mrs. Schofield interrupted. "Is the Dowager Lady Gold coming to visit, by chance?"

"As a matter of fact, she is with me already."

"How wonderful. Please do tell her I'll call when I'm back from my appointment."

"I will. She'll be delighted."

Ginger excused herself. However, when she glanced back, she caught eyes with Lieutenant Schofield. He was watching her as she knew he would.

Back in the kitchen, Ginger gave Boss over to Lizzie. "Do you have that list of fine dress shops your former employer liked to visit?" she asked.

"Yes, madam. I nearly forgot." Lizzie dug through her skirt pockets and produced a folded piece of notepaper. "Mrs. Thornton helped me to remember the names of some of the places."

Ginger glanced over the list. "Thank you. It's a good start."

Lizzie bobbed and whisked Boss away. Ginger was grateful that the girl liked animals.

Felicia was nowhere to be seen, however Ambrosia was nursing a pot of tea in the sitting room. Ginger told her about the Schofields.

"My word!" Ambrosia's hand went to her heart. "She's going to call?"

"Grandmother, is there a problem?"

"She's just so … finicky. She always has the best of everything, you know. The best clothes, the finest furnishings, the best advice. Even though I have a title! It's unnerving."

"I didn't realise."

"She can be quite nosy, too. I'm surprised it's taken her this long to interfere."

"I'm sorry, Grandmother. She invited herself. I thought you might like the company. She seemed excited to see you."

Ambrosia shifted nervously, and put her teacup on the tabouret. "Of course, she's excited to see me. She can't wait to rub it in. Oh, my." She fiddled with her full, pleated skirt. "Mrs. Schofield's going to look down her nose at my dress."

"You look lovely," Ginger said consolingly. "Remember, you are the Dowager Lady Gold. You look down *your* nose at her."

Ginger had never thought she'd invoke a title before, but she was concerned at how ruffled the older woman had become.

"Quite right, quite right. Thank you, Ginger." Ambrosia stood and leaned on her walking stick. "I need to change. How might I procure this Lizzie?"

"I'll get her for you, Grandmother."

Ginger tasked Lizzie to help Ambrosia and to send Felicia her way should she run into her. That girl! Ginger would leave without her if she didn't materialise soon. As if Felicia could sense that Ginger was about to abandon her, she burst on the scene dressed in a dark, pleated skirt, contrasting white blouse and a colourful scarf tied around her neck.

"I'm ready whenever you are, Ginger!" she said as she slipped into an oversized autumn jacket and set a straw hat adorned with purple feathers on her head. "I've got plenty of ideas on how we can spruce up the old place. Let's bring Hartigan House into the twentieth century!"

"I'd love to hear your ideas," Ginger said. "Let's go."

In the Daimler, Ginger explained. "Before we visit the decor shops, I would like to drop into a few dress lounges."

"Lounges?" Felicia said. "That sounds hoity-toity."

"It is, however, I would like to introduce myself to the fashion designers and personal shoppers. In case I'm in need of a hoity-toity gown one day."

Felicia laughed. "I like how you think, sister!"

Felicia didn't seem at all perturbed by Ginger's driving. Proof that it was Haley's problem, not hers. Ginger watched her sister-in-law from the corner of her eye.

"How are you doing, Felicia? Really?"

"How do you mean?"

"Are you happy?"

"Of course!" Felicia smacked her cherry-red lips. "I'm one of the *bright young things*!"

Ginger smiled. "That you are."

"If you mean am I happy about being stuffed away in dreary old Bray Manor, then the answer is an unequivocal no."

"Surely it can't be that bad?"

"There's just not enough money, Ginger. I mean that in the most respectful way. It's like a gigantic tomb. We hardly have more staff than you. And I'm quite serious about there being no men."

"Yes, the manor could use a man about to look after things."

"Well, I wasn't talking about *those* kind of men," Felicia winked, "but yes, workmen, too."

"I'd like to come soon," Ginger said. "To visit Daniel's grave."

Felicia sobered. For once she had nothing to say.

Ginger reached over to squeeze her hand. "We both lost a tremendous amount when he died. We can make it through together."

"He's been dead for five years. I got on quite all right without you."

Ginger felt slapped by the anger behind the words.

"I'm sorry I didn't come sooner."

Felicia's mask of joy returned. "Let's not talk about the past, shall we." She pointed. "The Ritz Hotel! How fabulous it would be to stay there one day. Ginger, you're so lucky to be so close to everything. I absolutely adore London!"

Ginger continued through Mayfair, and as good fortune would have it, she found a place to park directly in front of one of the shops just off Regent Street.

"Providence!" Ginger said brightly. Best to keep the mood light.

The lounge assistant was tall and thin, and wore a plain black suit. Though she wore spectacles, it was clear she scanned and then assessed Ginger and Felicia by what they wore. Ginger had felt confident in her Vionnet, until now anyway. Once again she invoked her title.

"Hello, I'm Lady Gold, and this is my sister-in-law Miss Gold. I'm newly arrived in London, and I'm making my acquaintance with all the finest lounges in the city. I've yet to order my autumn wardrobe, you see."

That produced a graceful and slightly apologetic smile. "Zat explains why I've not seen you before, madam. I'm Madame Jardin. Please, come zees way."

Ginger didn't have to pretend to be delighted by the latest designs from the greatest Parisian fashion designers of the day such as Madeleine Vionnet, Edward Molyneux, and Jeanne Paquin.

Felicia became so excited, Ginger worried she might hyperventilate.

"As you can probably tell, my sister and I have a great enthusiasm for fashion. I'm actually looking for a particular dress. I remember it from the last time I visited in 1913. Stunning. Maybe it was purchased from this lounge. Were you here then?"

"So long ago? Well, yes, I was here. Tell me about *zees* dress."

Ginger described the gown found on the skeleton. "I'm pretty sure it's a Lucile."

Madame Jardin clicked her tongue and shook her head. "I'm afraid I don't know ze dress. I would've remembered zat."

Ginger and Felicia made their excuses to leave with Ginger promising to come again.

"What was that about?" Felicia asked.

"I'm curious about a particular dress. Nothing more."

They visited two more lounges with the same results.

—

"You must tell me what is so important about this dress," Felicia said as they approached their fourth store. "Either that, or make a purchase!"

Ginger stopped on the pavement outside the entrance and considered Felicia's request. It seemed unwise to fill her head with scary stories about a skeleton found in the attic. Before she could come up with a reasonable ruse, a man's voice interrupted them.

"Lady Gold!"

"Inspector Reed? What are you doing here?" Ginger wondered briefly if Basil Reed had had the same idea to interview the fashion lounges—she certainly hoped not. He'd never be allowed entrance.

"I've come to find you. Your maid Lizzie said you were visiting the shops. She gave me a list."

Ginger frowned. What on earth could merit such a personal errand?

"What is it, Inspector?"

Basil Reed released the newspaper pinched under his arm and opened it to reveal the front page. "I'm afraid the crime has been leaked to the press."

The headline of the *Daily Mail* read:

REMAINS OF UNKNOWN WOMAN FOUND IN ATTIC OF WESTMINSTER HOME

Home to the Hartigan family for nearly three decades, the house has been left empty as widower Hartigan moved to America in 1901 with his young daughter to wed Miss Sally Withers, an American. Mr. Hartigan is recently deceased and his daughter Georgia Hartigan, now Lady Georgia Gold, returned to London to claim her inheritance whence the ghastly discovery was made.

Ginger gasped. *"Oh, mercy.* This can't be good for your investigation."

"Ginger," Felicia demanded, "what is this all about? It's just tabloid rubbish, isn't it?"

Ginger put a hand on Felicia's arm. "I'm afraid it's quite true."

"That's why you've been asking about that dress? It was found in the attic!"

Ginger admired Felicia's quick deduction but feared Basil Reed would be less impressed.

The inspector eyed her disapprovingly. "Have you been investigating, Lady Gold?"

She batted her eyes. "Just asking a few questions, Inspector. I'm sure it can't hurt."

Basil Reed let out a frustrated breath. "We can talk about this later. The reason I'm here is to escort you both home. I'm afraid there's rather a mob of reporters camped out in front of your gate."

CHAPTER ELEVEN

GINGER FOLLOWED BEHIND Basil Reed's unmarked forest-green 1922 Austin 7.

"Oh my word!" Felicia said as they approached the house. Situated near the front gate, a cluster of men in suits and hats carried cameras and camera gear. "You're famous!"

Ginger grimaced. "This is the kind of fame I can do without."

Basil Reed turned down the alley to the back of Hartigan House. The garden wasn't exempt and a crowd of journalists waited in the alley expectantly. Basil Reed stepped out and flashed his badge at the men, instructing them to step back from the property and to make way.

"Or I'll arrest you for trespassing," he added for the benefit of the stragglers.

He then opened the garage for Ginger and Felicia, waited for Ginger to park and then escorted them through the garden to the kitchen. Flash bulbs went off frenetically, reminding Ginger of the Fourth of July.

"I feel like a film star!" Felicia said.

The reporters began to shout out questions.

"Do you know who the victim is?"

"How'd you come across the body?"

"Lady Gold, are you staying in London?"

The trio made it through the kitchen door with Basil shutting it firmly behind them just as the last question was asked. "Lady Gold, did you know about Mr. Hartigan's …."

Ginger blanched. *Mr. Hartigan's what?* The police didn't know about her father's instructions to keep the door locked, so that bit of information hadn't been leaked. She wished desperately that she had heard the end of the question.

"Who was that reporter?"

"Which one?" Basil asked. "There are dozens out there."

"The one who asked the last question?"

Basil Reed shook his head. "I'm sorry, I didn't see him."

Ambrosia heard them arrive and waddled towards them furiously once they entered the dining room. "Oh, thank the good Lord you're back! This invasion of privacy is simply dreadful! Please do tell, Ginger, what on earth is going on? And who is this gentleman?"

"Grandmother, do calm down. This is Inspector Reed. Inspector Reed, the Dowager Lady Gold."

Basil Reed removed his hat. "It's a pleasure to meet you."

Ambrosia was too flustered to engage in social niceties. "Inspector? Ginger, has a crime been committed?

Ginger corralled the distressed woman into the sitting room. "Let's have some tea, and I'll explain everything. Everything is going to be all right." Her voice soothed, but in her heart, she wasn't certain it would be true. Fear that irreparable damage would come to her father's name gripped her with a black fist.

The facts of the situation could no longer be withheld under the circumstances, and Ginger intended to round up all the members of the Hartigan House household into the sitting room to explain.

However, she hadn't anticipated company. She blinked back her surprise at the presence of Mrs. Schofield and her grandson, Alfred.

"Oh my," Ginger said. "I'd forgotten you were dropping in." Mrs. Schofield stood to greet her and they loosely embraced. "So good to see you again. I do apologise for the circus outside."

"We'd only just arrived when the crowd appeared. So good that Alfred had assisted me inside."

"Hello again, Lieutenant Schofield."

"Please do call me Alfred."

"Alfred." She didn't extend an invitation in kind. "Such providence that you are here for your grandmother."

She waved at Basil Reed. "This is Chief Inspector Reed from Scotland Yard."

To Basil she said, "Certainly there must be a way to escort the Schofields home. They only live next door."

"If it's possible to stay on private property, there is. Is there access through the back garden?" he said.

"I believe there is, though it may be grown over. Pippins?"

The butler, who waited quietly to the side by the doorway, stepped forward. "Madam?"

"Please see to the pathway, and clear it if possible."

"Yes, madam," he said, then disappeared.

Ginger instructed Lizzie to refill the teacups. She then took a seat on the settee and motioned for Basil to sit on the other end.

Felicia flopped into an empty chair. "This day just gets better and better. We never have any excitement at Bray Manor. It's frightfully dull."

"I'll take dull any day!" Ambrosia said. She sat upright on the edge of her seat and sipped her tea. The china cup rattled on the saucer, evidence of her nerves.

"I, for one, am more than curious," Alfred said. He stoked the fire before leaning against the mantel in what Ginger thought was a pretentious pose. He ducked his chin to gain a view out of the window. "Pray tell, what has caused this uproar of camera-toting fellows."

Ginger shared a look with Inspector Reed who cleared his throat before speaking.

"I can only tell you what the press already knows. Regretfully, Lady Gold made a grisly discovery upon her recent arrival. Remains of a woman's body were found in the attic."

The news, so shocking, caused the room to go immediately silent. Ambrosia nearly dropped her teacup, which thankfully was empty, and set it down with a rattle.

"You can't be serious," she finally said.

Felicia squealed, "It's so scandalously delicious!"

"Do be quiet, child!" Ambrosia snapped.

Mrs. Schofield's white bony fingers fussed with the high collar of her blouse. "Oh my. Is it anyone we know?"

"We are still confirming the identity, madam," the inspector said.

Alfred whistled. "Blimey! How did she get nobbled?"

Ginger and Basil shared another look. Ginger was quite happy to let him share whatever news he deemed appropriate at this stage of his investigation.

Instead of answering he said, "Were either of you present at the soirée held here on the thirty-first of December 1913."

"1913?" Mrs. Schofield said. "What could that possibly have to do with the body in the attic?" She gasped. "Don't tell me it's been there for that long!"

"Just answer the question, please," Basil said.

Mrs. Schofield fiddled with her pearls. "Well, yes I was here. Mr. Schofield, my husband, was still alive. It was the last formal affair we attended before he passed away."

Alfred shook his head. "I was too young for such things."

"Does the name Eunice Hathaway ring any bells?"

Alfred shook his head, but Mrs. Schofield stared into

space as if digging up old files.

"Yes," she said. "She was the young lady on the arm of Lord Maxwell Turnbull. It was quite the scandal, you know, since Lord Turnbull had only been recently widowed and an appropriate time of mourning hadn't yet passed. Besides, she was a commoner and he was a Lord. The peerage was up in arms. It was in all the papers."

Ambrosia released a quiet derisive huff at the apparent slight to her class.

Mrs. Schofield eyed her slyly then continued. "Before too long Miss Hathaway was in her cups, as they say, always a glass of champagne in her hand, holding it high so everyone would see her ring."

"A ring?" Ginger said, thinking of the broken phalange.

"Yes. A tremendous ruby with four small diamonds around it. It quite dazzled in the electric lights, but how she flashed it about was simply off-putting. Everyone there had known Lady Turnbull. The young woman's behaviour was appalling."

Lizzie produced another hot pot of tea. Alfred took the moment to saunter over to Basil, hands in his trouser pockets.

"So mate, it's been a while, eh?"

Basil stood. "Indeed."

Ginger looked at the two men in surprise. "You know each other?"

"Indeed, we do," Alfred said. "Lieutenant Reed was in the same regiment as my brother—God rest his soul. Our old chap, Basil here, got invalided out before it was half over." He slapped Basil on the back, causing the inspector to wince. "Missed the best part at the end, you did," Alfred continued. "Lucky you."

"You're pretty lucky too, I'd say," Basil said. "You're here and standing."

Alfred chuckled. "Righto. By the way, how's your wife? Emilia isn't it?"

Basil stiffened. "She's fine. What about your sweetheart? Sorry, I forget her name."

That produced a laugh. "I've already forgotten her name too, old chap!" He went to slap Basil again, but Basil sidestepped out of the way in time.

Felicia had disappeared and returned with freshly applied make-up. Red lipstick outlined rosebud lips, and her eye shadow was far too dark for the time of day. She approached Alfred and giggled at him flirtatiously. "Am I to understand you live next door?"

Alfred smiled in return, his eyes scanning her feminine form from her youthful face to her exposed ankles and her t-strap shoes. "I used to," he said. "Grandmother nursed me back to health after the war, and now I feel it's my duty to take care of her, so I drop in as often as I can."

"Oh, so sweet!" She batted her eyes. "A true gentleman."

"Grandmother's a good old bird."

Felicia stroked Alfred's arm. "You know London then, do you? You must take me around, show me the sights."

Ginger watched this interaction with alarm. She

didn't trust Alfred Schofield. Not in the least. "Felicia," she called. "Do me a favour, darling, and telephone the medical school. Ask for Miss Higgins and warn her about the excitement outside."

"Must I?" Felicia whined like a girl much younger than her actual age of twenty-one. "Can't you do it?"

Ginger kept her composure. "I would, but I must see to the Dowager Lady Gold and our guests. Pippins has the number."

"Then why can't he do it?"

"Felicia, child!" Ambrosia sputtered. "Has Ginger not done enough for you that you can't do one little thing in return!"

Felicia left with a huff, and at least for now, was safely out of Alfred Schofield's claws.

Pippins returned with news. "There are men loitering in the alley, but off the property. I opened the way next door with clipping shears. You can now quite easily cut through the gardens."

"Thank you, Pippins," Ginger said, feeling relieved. Their guests could soon depart.

"Alfred, darling," Mrs. Schofield said loudly. "Do help me out of the chair. Inspector, will you escort us?"

CHAPTER TWELVE

THE NEXT DAY Ginger drank her mid-morning tea on the veranda in the garden. Who knew how long the weather would remain nice enough to sit outside in the sun? Boss, in agreement, sprawled his small black and white form across the warm flagstones.

Ambrosia and Mrs. Thornton were working together in the garden. The phrase *working together* was a bit generous. Ginger watched them from under the rim of her hat.

"Mrs. Thornton, you've really got to manage the blackberries," Ambrosia said as she rested against her walking stick. "If you're not careful, they'll take over the whole garden. Such a shame they weren't harvested this summer. Think of all the pies that could've been made with all the berries on the ground. And those ripe belladonna berries make a mess when trodden upon. They should be picked soon and destroyed. The plant should be removed. Such a thing isn't suitable for a city garden. How did one get seeded here in the first place? And the ivy is quite out of control. Before too long, you shan't be able to see the fence."

"Why doncha keep to the roses you like so much, Dowager Lady Gold," Mrs. Thornton said with noticeable irritation in her voice. "I'll take care of the rest."

"At Bray Manor we have a groundskeeper to tend to the garden."

"'Ow nice for ya, madam."

Ambrosia tsked. "He never lets things get away like this."

"'Artigan 'Ouse 'as been unattended for some time, madam. Perhaps 'e'd like to visit us 'ere and 'elp us out."

"Oh my, no. Bray Manor keeps him busy enough."

The sound of the telephone bell resounded through the open window. Ginger heard Pippins answer. Soon afterward he entered the garden and announced. "Miss Higgins on the line for you, madam."

Ginger promptly left the two gardeners alone to continue their verbal sparring.

She held the candlestick telephone with one hand and held the earpiece to her ear. "Haley. Is everything all right?"

"Everything's the bee's knees, Ginger. You won't believe it, but *the body* is here in the medical lab."

"Our *body*? The bones?"

"Yes. Turns out that my professor, Dr. Watts, works closely with the inspector. He's his pathologist of choice."

"That's very interesting news," Ginger said. "Is it all right if I come over?"

"That's why I called, sugar."

Ginger had already walked Boss and was dressed for the day. She let Lizzie know she was leaving her pet behind and told Pippins where she was headed. After a three-quarter hour drive through busy morning traffic, she arrived at the London Medical School for Women.

She greeted Miss Knight and asked directions to the lab. Following the woman's instructions, Ginger was relieved to find Haley eating a sandwich as she waited for her in the hall.

"Finally," she said as she gobbled up the last bite.

"Traffic was atrocious."

Haley brushed the crumbs off her lap and led Ginger into the lab.

Without windows and lit by a scattering of bare bulbs, the room was rather gloomy. The linoleum on the floor was scuffed from gurney wheels and rubber-soled shoes. All the surfaces and apparatuses were a bland, white ceramic. The remains of the body were spread out on the table with all the fabric and dried flesh removed.

"Normally the bodies that come through here have flesh and blood along with the bones," Haley said. She pointed to what looked like large built-in filing cabinets. "The cadavers are stored over there. Thank goodness for electricity and refrigeration."

Ginger focused her attention onto the bones before her, laid out like a skeletal puzzle. "What do you make of them?"

Haley pointed to the area just beneath the jawbone. "The hyoid bone is broken. Dr. Watts says this points to strangulation as the cause of death."

"I see." Ginger paused, then asked, "What is Dr. Watts like?"

"He's intense. Very gifted."

"Do you have any female instructors?"

"A few, though I've heard the percentage of female professors is increasing over time."

Haley motioned to the skeleton on the table. "The bones are strong, and the sutures in the skull and palate are only partially fused, indicating youthfulness. There is evidence of a single break in the left ulna." Haley pointed to the forearm bone. "Take a look at this fracture line. Dr. Watts surmises it was from a childhood fall. The ribcage is free of nicks or fractures which points to an absence of abdominal trauma, either from a fist or stab wound. However, the phalanges of the right ring finger are damaged at the inter-phalangeal joint. The breakage must have occurred before the woman was abandoned in the attic. My guess is that someone had trouble removing a ring from our victim."

"I'm impressed, Haley," Ginger said. "I had no idea you could deduce so much from bare bones."

"I'm learning a lot from Dr. Watts."

Ginger hummed. "Indeed. Where is the good doctor?"

"He's been called to the hospital. I'm sorry you missed him."

"Another day, I'm sure," Ginger said. She rounded

the table to the other side, taking in all the evidence.

"Perhaps," Ginger said. She took a closer look at the skull and broken hyoid bone. "She had nice teeth," she said. "Probably a great smile."

Haley agreed. "A nice-shaped head too. No doubt she was attractive."

"No doubt."

"Have you confirmed that this is Eunice Hathaway?"

"As much as it is possible. Dr. Watt's mentioned that your neighbour Mrs. Schofield was brought to Scotland Yard. She confirmed the dress as the same one she saw Miss Hathaway wear."

Ginger leaned over the bones. "What led to your demise, Eunice? Who did this to you?"

CHAPTER THIRTEEN

LATER THAT AFTERNOON, Ginger sat in the office of Mr. William Hayes, solicitor. The building was in Whitechapel on the eastern edge of London City on a street that bordered the well-to-do and the not so well-to-do. It amazed Ginger how quickly neighbourhoods could change in such a short distance. In one, well-groomed streets filled with men in fine suits and top-hats and in the other, ditches dotted with rubbish and dirty youths scampering about suspiciously.

Mr. Hayes was a diminutive man with thinning hair and a weasel-like face. A pair of gold-rimmed *pince-nez* sat on a small upturned nose. The sturdy desk was crafted with good mahogany and designed to last for centuries, barring a woodworm invasion or fire. The large piece seemed to swallow the solicitor, causing him to appear as a child testing out his father's things.

This was the man Ginger's father had entrusted with the estate?

Ginger claimed the chair in front of the desk. She'd chosen a classic cream wool suit and white cloche for this meeting, wanting to look sophisticated and businesslike. Long white gloves reached her elbows and she folded her hands on her lap. "Thank you for seeing me at short notice, Mr. Hayes."

"No problem at all, Lady Gold. I was expecting you."

"Of course. Might I ask, how long have you worked for my father?"

Mr. Hayes tented his fingers and searched the ceiling. Ginger mistrusted him even more.

"I do believe he first came to me in thirteen. Yes, the autumn of 1913.

Again, the year 1913? "If you don't mind my asking, why did my father change solicitors that year?"

"Mr. Jenkins retired."

Simple answer. Too simple to be true? Ginger nodded and smiled. "1913 was the year I married Sir Daniel. We were wed in America but travelled here on our honeymoon in the summer. Unfortunately we never made it back for the winter soirée hosted by my father. I heard it was a delightful affair. Were you there?"

Mr. Hayes's finger tent opened, and collapsed, and opened again. "I don't recollect. That was ten years ago, so my memory is a little fuzzy."

"At any time do you recall meeting a woman named

—

Miss Eunice Hathaway?"

Pausing for a moment too long, he replied, "No. I'm afraid I do not."

The solicitor was lying.

"Do you attend a lot of soirées, Mr. Hayes?"

Annoyance registered on his face. "Hardly any at all."

"Then I'm surprised you don't remember this one? I heard Hal Sherman sang live. It was New Year's Eve."

"Yes, yes, Lady Gold. I remember now. Lovely event. But I confess, I'm not much for social dos.

This, Ginger believed.

"Was my father in some kind of trouble?"

William Hayes ceased his finger exercises and sat taller—as much as it was possible for a man his size to sit taller—in his expensive leather chair. "Why would you ask that, Lady Gold?"

Ginger raised a brow. "Why won't you answer the question?"

"I'm bound by confidentiality, even to the dead."

The solicitor's refusal to answer heightened Ginger's concern. As far as she knew, her father had been the epitome of hard work and integrity when it came to his businesses. He had been trusted and well-liked. Was it possible a man of his upstanding reputation had also carried terrible secrets to his grave?

Ginger experienced the light-headed sense of one walking a tightrope without a net. She pushed down her fears and recomposed herself. "What must I do to take care of my father's affairs?"

William Hayes pushed a stack of papers towards her

along with a fountain pen. "Simply sign where you see an X. Once I file with the city registrar, Hartigan House will be legally yours."

"Perfect. Do you mind if I take these home? I have a personal policy of not signing anything I haven't thoroughly read."

"Certainly, bring them back at your convenience." Mr. Hayes stood and Ginger found herself looking down at the man as she shook his hand.

"Good day, Mr. Hayes."

Ginger walked quickly down the street but slowed as she reached the Daimler. A group of dirty-faced boys with patches on their knees and holes in their shoes circled her motorcar. They rubbed grubby fingers on the windows as they looked inside.

"Hey!" Ginger shouted impulsively. Instead of scattering, they looked her up and down, and the largest kid, shoving hands in his pockets, scuttled over. "Looky 'ere, lads. Money inna dress."

"Now don't be disrespectful, young man," Ginger said. "Or I'll tell your mother."

The big boy laughed and the little ones joined in on his lead. "Tell me muhvah? I ain't got no muhvah."

The boys circled in closer and Ginger felt a wave of concern. "Allow me to reach my motorcar," she said.

"If ya could spare a few shillings, missus, we'll leave ya be."

Ginger huffed. "That's extortion."

The boy pressed up close, forcing Ginger to step back. "And that there's a pretty fancy word." She glanced around for assistance, but suddenly, the street seemed empty as if the boys had been given the stage.

"Let me get to my vehicle, and I'll give you what you want."

The circle opened, and Ginger passed by. She was thankful she'd thought to lock the door. She found change in her handbag, but before she gave it away, she said, "What are you going to do with this money?"

The larger boy dropped his grin. "The grocer just got a barrel of shiny new apples. I 'ave a little sister who ain't ate nuffin' all day."

Ginger's anger immediately ebbed and she handed out the coins, wishing there were more she could do. The boys left and she sat for a moment deep in thought when a tap at the window startled her.

The familiar face of a young waif with a dirty face and wearing a stained newsboy cap peered at her through the window.

"Scout?"

"Mrs. Gold. Is dat you?"

Ginger stepped out of the car and gave the small boy a hearty handshake.

"I know it's only been a few days, but it seems much longer," Ginger said. Scout had worked in the kennel with his older cousin on the SS *Rosa* when she crossed over from Boston.

"It does, missus." Scout stuffed small fists into the pockets of his tweed knickerbockers. "How's ol' Boss?"

"He's well. I have a mai—a girl at home who helps me to look after him now."

"Lucky 'er."

"How are Marvin and your uncle?"

"They's good. Hey, missus, I saw wat those lads did. I'm mighty sorry."

"It's not your fault for knowing them, Scout." As she did on the ship, Ginger had an overwhelming urge to swoop up the young boy and take him home. In her care he might have a decent chance at life. She'd even made him the offer, but he declined. As they say, blood is thicker than water.

"Are you going back to work on the *Rosa*?" she asked.

"Nah. Sumfin terrible happened to the captain, and the coppers and 'igher ups is all over it. Marvin says to stay put for now."

"I see." Ginger pulled out a five-pound note. "Take this and buy food for you, your cousin and your uncle."

"Oh, I couldn't missus. It woulda be charity."

"Think of it as a bonus for the extra love you gave to Boss."

Scout worked his lips wearily.

Before he could refuse, she added, "It's also a job."

The boy perked up. "Oh?"

"There's a man, a solicitor called William Hayes. His office is just over there."

"Short man wiv the kind of specs dat sit on the nose?"

"Yes, that man. Keep an eye on him. Don't let him see you, mind. Just if you …"

Scout grinned. "If I see sumfin 'spicious."

"Exactly."

"How do I find ya?"

"I'll be back a week today, around this time. I can meet you here."

Scout accepted the money. "Good ta see ya again, missus!"

CHAPTER FOURTEEN

"I BELIEVE THE KEY to this mystery lies in this list," Ginger said to Haley as they shared breakfast together in the morning room. With a polished fingernail, she tapped the sheet of paper Pippins had given her with the names of the soirée attendees from 1913. "Someone on this list knows what happened to Eunice."

Haley brushed crumbs from her mouth and sipped a strong, sweet, white coffee, thanks to Mrs. Thornton's willingness to brew it as instructed. "Dark like the French way," the cook had said with a tinge of disgust.

"Anyone standing out?" Haley asked.

"Well, Eunice came as Lord Turnbull's guest," Ginger said. "That makes him a person of interest.

According to the newspaper archives I found in my father's library, not only had Eunice arrived at the soirée with him, she was seen to leave with him as well. Turnbull swore to dropping her off in front of her flat building, which unfortunately, didn't have a doorman. It was just after one in the morning. After, he promptly went home; his arrival time was confirmed by his butler."

"So how did Eunice end up in the attic room of Hartigan House?"

Ginger tilted her head. "That's the big question, isn't it?"

Lizzie entered with Boss at her heels. "Are you ready for me to take away the dirties?"

"Yes, thank you, Lizzie," Ginger said, then patted her knees for Boss. "Come on, boy." Boss jumped onto Ginger's lap and nuzzled her chin before settling.

Ginger picked up the conversation once Lizzie left. "Mrs. Schofield didn't have anything nice to say about Eunice. One might gather that there were others who didn't appreciate her style, too."

"Have you had a chance to follow up on any of them?" Haley asked.

"Funny you should ask. As it happens, I have. Redecorating requires one to drive about, and I've taken opportunity to check up on most of them."

"Pray tell," Haley said.

"Lord and Lady Julian Brackenbury still live at the same elegant Westminster townhouse they lived in a decade ago. Their two sons have grown and left home. Lord Brackenbury has long since been a member of the House of Lords. I got that information from the scullery maid—it's a wonder how claiming to be an old family friend will get some tongues wagging."

"Lord Brackenbury is a man with some influence, then," Haley said.

Ginger nodded. "Indeed." She sipped her tea and continued. "Monsieur Gaston Moreau was a young man in 1913, barely twenty, though he'd already been promoted at his job at Barclays Bank. This is how he knew my father, and apparently, according to Pippins, Father was impressed with Monsieur Moreau's savvy investment advice. I'm told Monsieur Moreau has since married.

"Also on the list is Dr. Warren Longden, who continues to practice in Mayfair, Mr. Schofield Senior, now deceased, who came with Mrs. Schofield, and Lord Maxwell Turnbull, the one person I was unable to find new information on. He appears to be a regular guest in the penthouse room of the Ritz Hotel.

"Besides them, my father and Sally, and the staff which included Pippins, Mrs. Thornton and father's valet, Andrew Bailey."

"Who is now Lord Turnbull's valet, right?" Haley said.

"Right."

"That's an interesting twist."

"Indeed. Oh, there was also the solicitor Mr. William Hayes."

"Didn't you just visit him? Did it go well?"

Ginger was suddenly thankful that Haley lived at Hartigan House instead of the dorm. Otherwise they might never have a chance to chat and catch up like this.

"I saw him yesterday." She wrinkled her nose. "I'm not sure I trust him. It sounds unfair, but he just rubbed me the wrong way."

"Do you think he knows what happened to Eunice?"

"It's possible. As a solicitor, he has privilege and isn't required to tell the police."

Ginger went on to tell Haley about seeing Scout.

"Small world," Haley said.

"It was so good to see him. I'm really fond of the little man."

"He's found a good friend in you, Ginger."

"I think we've found a good friend in each other."

"So what's your plan now?" Haley asked. "Are you going to interview everyone on the list? If you are, I'd really like to go with you. Don't forget that one of them may be the murderer, and if they've killed once, they'll kill twice." She let out a low groan. "Oh, it's times like this I wish I wasn't so busy."

"It's fine, Haley. I can take Felicia if need be. Besides, I have a better idea."

"Oh? What's that?"

"I'm going to host a soirée and invite the names on the list."

"Interesting. What's the theme of the soirée? Why would they accept?"

"I'll call it a memorial party, in honour of my father. It would be utterly disrespectful for any of them not to attend."

"You will invite the inspector, won't you? Just in

case?"

"Of course."

Felicia entered the morning room just as Haley was preparing to leave.

"We're like ships in the night," Haley said.

Felicia yawned as she took an empty seat. "I'm just not a morning person."

Haley excused herself. "I don't want to miss my bus. Ginger, you'll call if you find out anything new?"

"I will. Have a good day!"

Felicia folded her arms on the table and rested her messy mop of auburn waves on them.

Ginger laughed. "Good thing Grandmother isn't here to see you. She'd find your laziness abhorrent."

"Where is the old girl?" Felicia mumbled.

"She's in the garden taking care of the roses."

Felicia pulled herself upright. "She's always messing around in the garden at Bray Manor, too. I supposed it's what keeps her fit. Is there tea?"

Ginger poured what remained in the pot into a clean cup. "I have a project for you."

Felicia glanced up suspiciously. "Oh?"

"I'm hosting a soirée."

"Really? How fun! When?"

"Next weekend. I need your help to redecorate quickly."

Felicia perked up, suddenly awake. "How delightful!"

Ginger called for Lizzie to replenish the breakfast for Felicia then produced the design books she'd picked up, slapping them onto the table. "We need new paint and wallpaper. You can help me choose."

Felicia thumbed through the books while she ate. Ginger took the opportunity to take Boss for a walk out the front gate and around the cul-de-sac. No sign of the Schofields today. When she returned, Boss found a comfortable chair beside the fireplace in the sitting room. Ginger gathered the design books and motioned to Felicia to follow her.

"We'll focus on the drawing room since that's where the soirée will be held," Ginger said. "We'll have time to attend to the sitting room and the rest of the house later."

The drawing room was three times the size of the sitting room, with heavily decorated walls and sun-bleached wooden floors. Satin curtains the colour of deep plum hung in long, heavy swaths framing the elongated windows. A glimpse of morning sunlight forked through in drastic, dusty rays.

"It's frightfully dull in here," Felicia said.

"New wallpaper will do wonders," Ginger said. "I'm picturing ivory white on the walls with grey paint on the floors. Do ask Lizzie to give this room a good dusting before we begin planning in earnest. We can all help to pack up the clutter."

There were several large paintings hanging on the walls, including a portrait of Ginger's parents from before she was born. Ginger stared at it wistfully. Her mother was so beautiful, her slender face framed with fiery red curls. Ginger recognised a resemblance that grew more pronounced as she herself aged. She felt an emptiness deep in her soul. Another loss. How different would her life be if her mother had lived?

The artist had expertly captured the vitality of youth in her father's eyes. Ginger only remembered him with thinner, greying hair. Her mother's sudden death had most certainly aged him.

A baby grand piano sat in the far corner and Ginger carefully lifted the lid. She played a C major scale and winced at the sour notes. "We must get this exquisite instrument tuned by the weekend. Felicia, can you ask Pippins to ring up a piano tuner?"

"Yes, I will." Felicia held up the wallpaper book against the wall, carefully studying each page before flipping to the next one. "What do you think of this?"

Ginger eyed the grey and cream geometric design. "Yes, along with new paint, it would look modern and divine."

"Would you like me to order it?"

"Please, do. And hire someone to put it up. This old stuff will need to be stripped first."

"So, who's invited to the soirée?" Felicia asked carefully. "Grandmama and I could stay a little longer."

Ginger smiled. "Of course you are welcome to attend. But to be truthful, it could turn out to be dangerous."

"Dangerous? How so?"

"You do recall the problem of the corpse in the attic?"

Felicia arched a brow. "How could I forget that!"

"Well, the dead woman's name was Eunice Hathaway, and her murder is still unsolved. The last time she was seen was the night of a soirée, hosted in this house by my father." Ginger paused. "I'm inviting the same people who were there that night."

"Ginger! You are an absolute brick! Of course I need to be there now. I'll be an extra set of eyes and ears."

"That would be helpful."

"May I ask, will the Schofields be there?"

Ginger held Felicia's gaze. "As it so happens Mrs. Schofield was an original attendee. She was with her husband then, but this time I do plan to include Lieutenant Schofield."

Felicia grinned. "That's splendid."

"Felicia dear, you must be careful. You know what they say about men."

"That they only want one thing?"

"That's right."

"Are you trying to be motherly to me Ginger? I quite have enough of that with Grandmama."

"I'm only trying to be sisterly," Ginger said. "Do be careful."

"I will. I just want to have a bit of fun before I'm old and grey. Hertfordshire is so frightfully drab."

"Here's something exciting," Ginger said, "I bought new furniture. It should arrive today or tomorrow."

"That *is* exciting! I can't wait to see it."

"Please do hang about in case it arrives today. Ask them to put the old things in one of the attic rooms."

Felicia winked. "But not *the* attic room."

"No, not that one, if you please."

"Where will you be?"

"I have errands to run.

Ginger sat in her father's study to make out the invitations. The room was masculine with dark wood panelling and corresponding desk and chair. Her father had spent many hours running his businesses from this room. And many evenings he had relaxed with a glass of spirits and a cigar in the library, most often with his nose in a book.

As she expected, Ginger found plain white card amongst her father's things, along with a working fountain pen. She carefully created a personal invitation for each person or couple on the list and sealed them in envelopes. She could give them to Pippins to post, but decided to hand-deliver them. She'd learn more about each suspect—for that was what they were—if she saw where they lived, and how they lived when not on display at a social event.

Ginger took the cards up to her room and slipped them into her handbag. She removed her day dress and donned her ivory wool suit. It said, *take me seriously*. She said goodbye to Boss before heading for the garage.

"Lord Turnbull," she said to herself, "here I come."

CHAPTER FIFTEEN

GINGER HEADED towards the Ritz and realised in time that she was about to pass Dr. Longden's house, and swung in sharply—protesting horns notwithstanding. The surgery was located only a short walk from the doctor's residence, and the fact that patients were walking into it prompted Ginger to pull up in front.

The waiting room was full of people who glanced up briefly as Ginger entered before returning their attention to their magazines and newspapers. She approached the receptionist who stood studiously over an opened file cabinet.

"Would it be possible for me to see Dr. Longden?"

"Do you have an appointment?"

"No, uh," Ginger read the name card on the desk,

"Miss Bird. I'm not in ill health. He's a friend of my family and I have something to tell him."

"You should arrange to meet him outside of office hours, madam," Miss Bird said mid-file. "He's very busy today."

"Yes, I see that. Could you tell him Lady Gold was here?"

The receptionist paused in her filing. "Gold? I don't recall the name."

"Gold is my married name. My family name is Hartigan. George Hartigan was my father."

Miss Bird finally gave Ginger her attention. "Yes, I remember Dr. Longden mentioning the loss of a patient who died in America. Boston, wasn't it?"

"It was."

A nurse entered the waiting room and called for the next patient as another having just seen the doctor, left the surgery.

"I'm sorry, but he really is very busy today. Would you like me to give him a message?"

Ginger relented. "Here's an invitation." She handed Miss Bird the card. "It's for a memorial party in my father's honour. I'm sure Dr. Longden will want to be there."

Miss Bird held the invitation firmly in one hand. "I'll be sure to give it to him."

Ginger hadn't any doubt that the serious woman would do just that.

Her next stop, the Ritz. As expected, she had trouble getting information from the man at the desk. Even her title didn't hold much punch with him. Feeling exasperated,

Ginger was about to leave the invitation with the pouchy man, when Lord Turnbull himself stepped out of the lift. An L-shaped scar on his tall forehead marred his handsome facial features. His dark hair combed neatly to the side, was shiny from brilliantine. Ginger knew the man was the one she sought because she recognised her father's former valet, Andrew Bailey, walking one step behind him.

"Lord Turnbull!"

The man stopped and turned toward Ginger. He smiled when he took her in, obviously pleased with what he saw.

"And who, may I ask, is addressing me?"

"I'm Lady Gold." She held out a gloved hand and Lord Turnbull made a show of kissing it.

"Pleased to meet you, Lady Gold. How can I help?"

"I believe you knew my father, George Hartigan." Ginger carefully watched the reactions from both men: Andrew Bailey's eyes rounded at her father's name. Lord Turnbull stiffened before forcing the return of his smile.

"Yes, of course. Our paths crossed once in a while through business."

An understatement. Ginger knew that Lord Turnbull and her father had in fact been business *partners*.

"You must've heard that he passed away last year?"

"No. I hadn't heard. How sad."

The way his mouth twitched slightly when he spoke caused Ginger to wonder at the truthfulness of this statement. Lord Turnbull was doing his best to distance himself from George Hartigan. Why?

"My deepest condolences, Lady Gold."

"Thank you, Lord Turnbull. The reason I've called on you is to give you this." She handed him his invitation. "I request your presence at a memorial party for my father."

"I see." Lord Turnbull's dark eyes moved from the card to Ginger's face. He smiled stiffly. "I'm afraid that shan't be possible."

Ginger grabbed at his arm. "Oh, you must! It won't be a large gathering, just a few who knew my father. Like Mr. Bailey! Surely, as my father's former valet, he would want to be there, and he can't possibly come if you don't, Lord Turnbull."

Lord Turnbull struck Ginger as the type of man who found it hard to say no to women—at least she hoped so. She made sure to keep strong eye contact and smiled widely. "Please. You can even bring a companion if you like."

"Perhaps I'd like to make you my companion?"

Ginger laughed. "I'd love that, but unfortunately, I'll already be there with someone."

Lord Turnbull's mouth pulled up into a half-grin. Ginger perceived he was a man who liked a challenge. Nothing could be more entertaining than pursuing a woman who was already taken.

"I'll most certainly attend, Lady Gold."

"Fabulous." She squeezed his arm and winked. "The party wouldn't be the same without you."

Ginger's next stop was Monsieur and Madame Moreau. Monsieur Moreau showed extreme gratitude at the invitation. Unfortunately, Madame Moreau was away shopping. "I can't wait for you to meet her," he said.

"I look forward to it," Ginger replied. She believed she had good intuition and insight into people and found that Monsieur Moreau appeared genuine. No guile or secrets, just honest emotion.

Lord and Lady Brackenbury were quite the opposite. Ginger had to break through two rounds of servants before she was finally granted an audience. The couple was older, near retirement age, and obviously well set in their ways. It was clear that Ginger was upsetting their routine.

"So sorry to intrude," Ginger said warmly. "I'm Lady Gold, daughter of George Hartigan."

Lady Brackenbury turned to her husband and spoke loudly, "Who?"

Lord Brackenbury removed a pipe from his mouth and spoke loudly in return. "George Hartigan's daughter."

"George?"

"He's the fellow who died abroad."

"He died?"

Lord Brackenbury nodded at his wife, then turned to face Ginger. "I'm sorry. My wife's hearing is going, along with her memory." He slid the pipe back into his mouth, though Ginger was quite certain the instrument wasn't lit.

"I understand," she said. "Father passed away last summer before he could return to London to say goodbye to his friends. I'm hosting a memorial party in his honour and would love you to come."

Lord Brackenbury frowned. "We didn't really know your father that well …"

"There won't be very many people there, and quite

honestly, I don't know many of Father's London friends and acquaintances. I found your names in his diary." A half-truth. "It would mean so much if you could come. No need to stay long."

Lord Brackenbury sighed, removed the pipe, and then conceded. "Lady Brackenbury does like a party. It's been a while since I've taken her anywhere. All right then, we'll come."

Lady Brackenbury tapped her husband's arm. "What?" she shouted.

"We're going to a party!"

"A party?"

"Yes!"

Lady Brackenbury smiled. "I do love a good party."

Ginger left the Brackenburys and inwardly celebrated her success. Outside of Dr. Longden, she had met each one in person. She really didn't know what to make of Lord and Lady Brackenbury, or quite understand their connection to her father. Ten years makes a big difference at their age. They were likely both a force to reckon with a decade earlier.

Ginger had one more stop to make before she needed to get home and assist in the redecorating efforts. She pulled into the parking area at the back of Scotland Yard. Using the rear-view mirror, she took a moment to reapply her lipstick and adjusted her cloche. Satisfied that she looked her best, she exited the motorcar in search of Basil Reed.

She found him in his office. She'd been there enough times now that the constable at the front desk simply waved her through. Basil Reed stood when he saw her standing in the doorway. Ginger sashayed to the empty chair and claimed it, crossing her legs with flair.

The inspector cleared his throat and sat behind his desk. "Lady Gold. To what do I owe this pleasure?"

"I'm throwing a party and I wanted to extend a personal invitation."

Basil Reed couldn't suppress a grin. "Thank you, but I really am quite busy. Solving crimes and such."

"Oh, Inspector, I'm aware. That's why you'll be pleased to know that this is a working party."

Basil's brow furrowed in a way that was becoming a common occurrence when he considered her. "What do you mean?"

"I mean, that for my guests, it's a party, but for you and me, it's work."

"I'm afraid I still don't understand. Especially since work for me is quite different than work for you."

Ginger pressed on. "In this instance, I think we can agree to disagree. But you simply must attend."

"Why must I, Lady Gold?"

Ginger arched a brow, and her green eyes sparkled. "Because I've invited *the list*."

"The list?"

"Yes. The guests who attended my father's final soirée ten years ago."

"Mrs. Gold, I must protest!"

Ginger noticed how he slipped out of her title, reverting to the address she'd introduced herself as when they met on the SS *Rosa*.

"You can protest all you like, Mr. Reed," She responded in kind. "I intend to find out what happened to Eunice Hathaway." And, she thought, to find out the truth about her father's involvement. "You'd be wise to accept my assistance. I'm going to proceed either way."

"You are an exasperating woman."

"Thank you."

"In that case, I will accept your invitation."

"Fabulous." Ginger rose to leave. At the door, she glanced over her shoulder and said, "Will Mrs. Reed be with you?" She was more than a little curious about the elusive Mrs. Reed. Who was this woman who appeared to have abandoned such a fine man as Chief Inspector Basil Reed?

A shadow flickered behind Basil's eyes. "I'm afraid not."

Ginger hummed. "It's probably for the best, this time around."

"Why do you say that?"

"Because Lord Turnbull wanted me to be his guest, and I told him I couldn't because I was already attending with someone. I'd ask Lieutenant Schofield, but that would break Felicia's heart." Ginger's green eyes twinkled. "That leaves you."

CHAPTER SIXTEEN

A WEEK HAD FLOWN BY for Ginger as she oversaw the work being done in the drawing room. New paint and paper on the walls and new furniture around the large brick fireplace freshened the place immensely. There were a few things left to do, but mostly she had to finalise plans with Pippins and Mrs. Thornton for the soirée.

Ginger was pleased to note that her left-side driving skills had improved after so many trips to and fro in the city. She'd been accustomed to the sounds of noisy horns directed her way, yet today, there had only been a few. She'd even had reason to squeeze the rubber ball section of the horn, which was secured to the exterior of the window frame. Quite thrilling.

Her eyes darted to the document Mr. Hayes had

given her. She had read it thoroughly, and if the solicitor intended on behaving unscrupulously towards her, he wasn't using this contract to do it.

Mr. Hayes once again sat in his overly big chair looking small. His physical size didn't represent the level of his intelligence.

"How do you do," she said when she entered his office. Mr. Hayes rose to greet her and shook her hand. "Lady Gold. I trust you found everything in order?"

Ginger sat daintily in the chair opposite William Hayes, crossed her ankles and retrieved the document from her handbag. "Everything appears to be in order," she said as she slid the papers across the desk. "You'll find my signature on the last page."

William Hayes thumbed through the document until he landed at the end and studied Ginger's signature.

His fingers found each other and tented. "Mrs. Georgia Hartigan Gold," he said with a grin.

"That's me!"

"Good, well, I'll file these with the city. Mr. Hartigan's banker will ring you to officially sign over your father's accounts."

"Thank you, Mr. Hayes, for taking such care of my father and his affairs."

"You are most certainly welcome, Lady Gold. And I continue to be at your service."

"Brilliant. And as my solicitor, you must attend the soirée I'm throwing this weekend. A memorial party in honour of my father."

"Oh, I don't know ..."

"Mr. Hayes, you simply must. I know you don't favour social events, but even you must admit that meeting people in person is good for business. I'm sure many of my guests might be in need of legal advice at some point."

The solicitor's fingers stilled. "I suppose you do have a point."

"It's settled then," Ginger said. She handed him his invitation. "This makes it official."

Ginger said goodbye to the solicitor then strolled casually to her motorcar. She scoured the street in search of young Scout.

Just as she approached the boot of the Daimler, he popped out of nowhere like she'd known him to do,

"Missus," he called.

Ginger waited for him to approach. "Hello, Scout. How are you?"

"Just fine, missus, just fine."

"Good to hear it. How was 'work' this week?"

"I saw sumfin 'spicious, missus."

"Oh?"

"Your solicitor got 'imself into a row with a tall man in a bowler 'at. The gent looked to be summon important like."

"How bad was the row? Loud talking? Did you hear what they said?"

"No, missus. But they come to cuffs. The short one almost fell 'ead over ears, 'e did."

"Oh dear. Did you notice anything unique about the tall man?"

"Oi, yes, missus. 'E 'ad a scar like this on 'is

fore'ead." Scout place his fingers in the shape of an L on his own small head. "I saw it in the lamplight."

Turnbull. He not only knew Hayes, but they had had words. Things could get interesting if they both showed up at the soirée.

"Thank you, Scout. This is most helpful." Ginger handed him four shillings. "Consider this a retainer, should I need your assistance in the future."

"Thank ya, missus," he said with a toothy grin. "I is yer man!"

Ginger patted him on the head. "Yes, you are."

She had plenty to think about on her way home: Hartigan House was officially her house. She, Ginger Gold, owned a large London home in a prestigious area. "Thank you, Father," she whispered. No longer simply a visitor, she was a London resident. After such a short time away from Boston she felt entirely British—which she was, as her birth certificate and passport proved—and the sensation caused her a measure of consternation.

For over twenty years Ginger had seen herself as American. When she thought of Boston her heart squeezed with homesickness. Having two homes conversely made her feel like she had none. Was she British or American? Should she stay in London, or go back to Boston as planned?

She could admit to missing her sister, Louisa, a little bit, but not her stepmother in the slightest. She and Sally had spent the first few years in Boston butting heads and vying for her father's attention. That cooled when Louisa was born. Ginger's desires for adventure skewed more towards what was happening with her friends and colleagues outside of the house, rather than the squawking child inside. Over time it was clear that unspoken lines had been drawn—Sally and Louisa on one side and Ginger and George on the other. It was quite likely that the welcome mat in front of the brownstone's front door would be whisked away upon hearing of Ginger's return.

"Pippins," Ginger called out as she entered Hartigan House. It occurred to her that she hadn't asked Pippins and Mrs. Thornton, who were both present at the winter soirée, if they knew anything about Miss Eunice Hathaway. You never knew what little detail might prove to be the thing to break a case wide open.

Pippins materialised in the sitting room as Ginger removed her coat and gloves. "Hello, Pips. Might I ask you a couple of questions regarding the final soirée hosted here by my father?"

"Certainly, madam."

"Do you remember a Miss Eunice Hathaway in attendance? She wasn't on the list."

"Oh yes. The guest of Lord Turnbull. A … *vivacious* young woman. She was a surprise for us all."

"Did you not like her?"

"I didn't know her well to have an opinion." The butler's gaze rested on Ginger. "But …"

"But?"

"I do believe Mrs. Thornton and Miss Hathaway were acquainted."

"Did Mrs. Thornton tell you this was so?"

"No, madam. It was more in the way they interacted

together. Staff is used to being ignored and unseen, and indeed, Miss Hathaway looked through the lot of us working that night…"

"Except Mrs. Thornton?"

"Yes, madam. I caught the two of them smiling at each other, just softly, mind you. Not in a way anyone else would notice."

"I see. Thank you, Pips. Would you mind fetching Mrs. Thornton for me."

"Yes, madam. Er, you won't mention that I …"

"I promise not to attach your name to my inquiry. I'm simply interviewing all the staff who were present that night."

Mrs. Thornton entered the sitting room a few minutes later, her round face flushed red at being summoned. Ginger hurried to set the woman's mind at ease.

"Mrs. Thornton, I have a question for you, nothing urgent, just a curiosity of mine I hope you can relieve."

"I'll do my best to 'elp ya, madam."

"You might've heard about the tragic discovery in the attic."

"Yes, madam. It's been quite exciting news below." By below, Ginger knew that Mrs. Thornton wasn't only referring to the three staff at Hartigan House, but in the servant community in Kensington and probably all of London. She kept a friendly expression despite the distaste she felt.

"Are you familiar with the name Miss Eunice Hathaway?"

Mrs. Thornton's red face instantly became dangerously pale. She reached for the back of one of the chairs. "I'm sorry madam," she explained. "I've been unwell."

"Do you need a glass of water?"

"No, I'm quite all right now."

"You're sure?"

"Yes, madam." The cook swallowed. "I did know Miss 'Athaway. I worked at the 'Athaway residence for many years, before I came to work at 'Artigan 'Ouse the first time. Watched the young lady grow up, I did. We were all simply shattered when she went missing."

The telephone rang and Ginger listened to ascertain if Pippins was going to get it or if she needed to make a dash. Since the phone ceased ringing she surmised that Pippins had answered.

Pippins entered the sitting room moments later. "Telephone for you, madam."

"Do you need anything more from me, madam?" Mrs. Thornton asked.

"That's fine for now," Ginger said. She quickly walked to the telephone in the morning room and picked up the candlestick receiver. "Hello?"

"Lady Gold? This is Chief Inspector Reed."

Full official title. Not a casual call. Ginger's stomach tensed. "Well hello, Inspector. I was just thinking of you."

"You were? Well, you can tell me why in a moment. I promised I'd call with any news of the case." He paused and Ginger sensed his reluctance.

"Yes, what is it?"

"I received Dr. Watts's report. His lab analysed the fabric strip found in your motorcar. Dr. Watts says it's a match to the dress worn by Eunice Hathaway."

CHAPTER SEVENTEEN

EVERYTHING CAME TOGETHER for the soirée as planned. Though Ginger would have liked to have renovated the entire house, she was pleased with the transformation of the drawing room over such a short time. The deep burgundies found in the upholstery and curtains were replaced with lighter shades of rose. The walls were painted and papered with themes of ivory, grey and mint-green. There were far fewer pieces of furniture and accessories, yet enough to house a gathering of this size comfortably. Lizzie had arranged the candle lighting to perfection while Mrs. Thornton's addition of vases filled with her garden wildflowers added to the relaxed atmosphere, giving the room a light floral scent.

"Pippins," Ginger said. "Would you mind putting on

a record?"

Pippins nodded subtly. "Of course, madam."

Soon the gramophone filled the room with the Paul Whiteman orchestra.

"Marvin," Ginger said, calling out to her temporary waiter, "you look dashing in that uniform."

It had been Ginger's idea to employ Scout and his older cousin Marvin for the night. Pippins and Mrs. Thornton showed their disapproval and doubt in Ginger's common sense with carefully worded and emotionally toned-down expressions of caution. Ginger had insisted that she trusted these boys and her loyal staff accepted her decision gracefully.

"Thank ya, madam," the boy said. He was tall and lanky as many sixteen-year-old boys are. Ginger was pleased when Pippins had produced a suit in Marvin's size, once worn by a previous footman.

"It's your job to help Pippins with the drinks. Make sure the glasses are washed and dried."

The kitchen buzzed with energy. Mrs. Thornton had Scout peeling vegetables. Ginger held in a smile that threatened to burst through as she watched him. Part of the job requirements was for Scout and Marvin to bathe. Marvin jumped at the opportunity. However Scout was quick to express his disapproval. Marvin dragged Scout into the bathing room, but his noises of dissent could be heard all the way down the hall.

"It smells scrummy, Mrs. Thornton," Ginger said.

"Thank you, madam. I 'ope you and your guests enjoy it."

"I hope it wasn't too much for you?"

"Pfft. This is a small affair."

There was a new face in the kitchen, a tall girl about Lizzie's age, with dark hair and large eyes. She bobbed when she saw Ginger.

"Hello," Ginger said. "Who might you be?"

"I'm Grace Duncan, madam."

Mrs. Thornton spoke up. "You told me to go a'ead and take on 'elp, madam."

"Of course. Welcome to Hartigan House, Grace."

Everyone had accepted the invitation: Dr. Longden, Mr. Hayes, Monsieur and Madame Moreau, Lord and Lady Brackenbury, Mrs. Schofield and Alfred Schofield, and Inspector Reed. Lord Turnbull telegrammed to say he'd be bringing a guest. With Ginger, Haley, Felicia and Ambrosia they numbered fifteen.

Ginger double-checked her reflection in the full-length mirror in the foyer. The sheer gold and emerald Callot Soeurs evening dress she wore sparkled in the light of the chandelier. She accented this with a delicate jewelled headband containing a featured emerald that rested on her forehead, and several ropes of pearls around her neck. Her favourite piece was the black feather boa draped elegantly over her shoulders.

Dressed this way, she really ought to be going out dancing and having a jolly time. If only this were a real party instead of a ruse to smoke out a killer. She wouldn't lose sight of that goal, especially with her father's reputation on the line.

Inspector Reed's pronouncement that the fabric strip

found in George Hartigan's motorcar was a match to the victim's dress was a blow. Her father was now personally tied to the case and there was nothing she could do about it. There was no way she would tell Basil Reed that her father had instructed Pippins to keep the door locked—that would only cast more doubt. She knew Pippins would remain discreet, though she couldn't expect him to lie under oath. *Oh mercy*, please do not let it come to that!

What was the relationship between George Hartigan and Eunice Hathaway? Miss Hathaway had been wearing an haute couture gown, which made sense since the Hathaway family, though not peerage, were highly respected and wealthy.

Mrs. Schofield remembered Eunice Hathaway wearing a large ruby ring on her finger. What happened to that? Had that been the motive for the crime? A mugging gone wrong?

"You're deep in thought."

Ginger startled at Haley's voice, then smiled at her friend. "Yes. This puzzle perplexes me."

"My mind has been meddling as well."

"Eunice Hathaway was seen leaving Hartigan House with Lord Turnbull. How did she then end up in the attic?"

"You're sure to know more by the end of the evening," Haley said encouragingly.

"That's the plan. By the way darling, you look divine."

Haley blushed. "I thought I'd put in a little effort for the cause. Lizzie lifted this from your wardrobe. I hope you don't mind."

The beaded ivory evening dress was the most feminine item Ginger had ever seen Haley wear. "Not at all. Indeed, I wish now I had invited an eligible bachelor. Come to think of it there are three unattached men joining us tonight."

"The doctor and the lawyer?" Haley said. "Aren't they ancient?"

"Well, yes. But there's also Lieutenant Alfred Schofield, though you might have to arm-wrestle Felicia for him."

"I think I'll take my chances on your next soirée."

Ginger laughed. "Yes, I believe there will be at least one more, though whether it's a housewarming party or a goodbye party is left to be seen."

"Ginger!" Ambrosia's high-pitched voice drew them both back to the sitting room.

"What is it Grandmother?" Ginger said. "Is something the matter?"

The matronly woman pointed upwards. "It's Felicia. She's wearing … well practically nothing at all! You must talk to her, Ginger. She simply won't listen to me. You'd think she was going out for a night of hedonistic dancing the way she's dressed. She'll bring scandal and shame down on your home. Oh, I should've taken her back to Bray Manor as planned before this dreadful idea of yours came to be. Really, a memorial soirée? Who's heard of such a thing?"

"Grandmother," Ginger said, guiding the woman to one of the wingback chairs. "Do calm yourself before you succumb to the vapours. I'll get you some tea."

"I'll do that," Haley offered, then added with a sly grin. "You go see to Miss Felicia."

Felicia was halfway down the stairwell when Ginger found her. Her sister-in-law wore a flashy sleeveless evening frock with narrow straps. The strands of beads she wore did little to cover the good amount of bare skin showing.

"Perhaps if you add a shawl, your grandmother's nerves will be spared."

"Must I?"

"I have the perfect one you can borrow. It's a Louise Boulanger."

Felicia followed Ginger and took a moment to pet Boss who was comfortably snoring on a padded chair. Ginger opened her wardrobe and disappeared inside. A few seconds later she presented a satin, art deco shawl with a foot-long fringe.

"Oh it is lovely," Felicia said as she draped it over her shoulders.

"And it looks lovely on you," Ginger said.

Felicia twirled in front of the mirror and sighed blissfully. "I believe Lieutenant Schofield will be pleased!"

"Oh Felicia."

"Just teasing, sister. I'll meet you downstairs. Ta ta."

Ginger breathed in the quiet of her room. She patted Boss. "You'll need to stay here tonight. Do let me know if someone enters who shouldn't be here." Her gaze settled on the photo of Lieutenant Gold on her night table, and she picked it up.

"My love, I don't know what's going to happen

tonight, but I do hope to get to the bottom of things once and for all. I wish you were here."

The door chimed. The first of her guests had arrived.

She set the photo back in its place. "Let the games begin."

CHAPTER EIGHTEEN

GEORGE HARTIGAN had a self-portrait painted when he turned thirty. It was said that he wanted to commemorate his early success as a businessman and that he thought it would impress future clients who visited him in his office.

When he turned forty, he scoffed at his own self-importance, and the painting was relegated to a short wall behind the door of his study. Ginger had it removed from there and hung prominently over the fireplace for this occasion.

Lady Brackenbury shouted her opinions to Ginger. "He was such a good-looking man. So sad about your mother. Oh dear, they're both gone now aren't they, darling?"

Ginger feared Lady Brackenbury might burst into tears. She turned the woman away from the painting and patted her frail hand. "It's quite all right, Lady Brackenbury."

"What?"

Ginger raised her voice. "It's quite all right!"

Ambrosia huffed. "Is she going to be yelling all night?" Ginger looked over Lady Brackenbury's head and gave her grandmother-in-law a pleading look. The Schofields arrived and Ambrosia could barely contain her look of offence when Mrs. Schofield took the seat beside her and said, "That's a nice turn-of-the-century frock, Dowager Lady Gold."

Felicia had attached herself to a dapper-looking Alfred Schofield, dressed smartly in a tuxedo jacket similar in style to those worn by all the men. She giggled and wrapped an auburn curl around one finger. Her charms appeared to be working on poor Alfred.

Inspector Reed stood just beyond by the drawing room door. His tuxedo jacket fit perfectly—black with shiny satin lapels, and a black bow tie on a bright white cotton shirt worn under a shiny white waistcoat. He wore formal trousers and black patent leather shoes, and looked every bit the member of the gentry he was. He grinned at Ginger in a way that made her knees give just a bit. She straightened her shoulders and marched over to him. "What do you think, Inspector?"

Basil Reed held a glass of gin rum cola that was mostly cola. Ginger knew this since she'd prepared the drink herself. The inspector had said he wanted to keep a clear head. She saw the wisdom in that and prepared a scotch and soda—mostly soda—for herself.

"It's a little early in the evening to say," Basil Reed responded. "I wonder when it will work it out that the guest list tonight matches the guest list from ten years ago."

"I hope not too soon." She laughed. "I'll have to instruct Pippins to keep the drinks going."

From her position by the fireplace, Ginger scanned the room. The Brackenburys sat together on the settee. William Hayes and Dr. Longden stood awkwardly next to the drinks trolley, each with one hand holding a drink, the other stuffed into a suit jacket pocket. Though they were engaged in conversation, neither of them looked the other in the eye. Ginger wondered what kind of history they shared.

The doorbell chimed again and Pippins went to answer it.

"It's either Lord Turnbull or Monsieur and Madame Moreau," Ginger said. "If it's Lord Turnbull, remember you're with me."

She nudged his arm, and he blinked hard. "I'll endeavour to do my duty."

Lord Turnbull entered with a flourish, removing his cloak and top hat and handing them to his valet. Ginger was glad to see Andrew Bailey there: she'd hoped Lord Turnbull would bring him.

Pippins slid in beside Ginger, his narrowed eyes darting to Bailey. "I hope you have your valuables locked up, madam."

There was an audible gasp when Turnbull entered the

drawing room. William Hayes blanched to an even paler shade of white. Lord Brackenbury said, "Oh, my."

Lord Turnbull presented his guest to Ginger. "Lady Gold, may I introduce Mrs. Harriet Fox."

Ginger's heart skipped a beat as she registered the redheaded woman before her. Though she had to be in her mid-forties, Harriet McCallum Fox retained her youthful beauty. The arrival of her father's former acquaintance, a rival to her mother, was a turn of events Ginger had not anticipated. She expertly kept her facial expression unreadable and welcomed her unexpected guest.

"Nice to see you again, Mrs. Fox," she said.

"Likewise."

It was Lord Turnbull's turn to be surprised. "You two are acquainted?"

Ginger smiled and answered before Harriet McCallum Fox could. "Mrs. Fox was a friend of my father's. I believe my stepmother was particularly fond of her. This is before Mr. Fox entered the picture."

Ginger's look conveyed the question. "Where is Mr. Fox?"

Harriet Fox scowled. "You're not the only one to lose a husband in the war. Now, do you mind if I get a drink?"

"Of course," Ginger said. She turned to Lord Turnbull. "I'm so glad you could make it. Might I introduce Mr. Basil Reed?"

Lord Turnbull smirked and shook Basil's hand. "So you're the one who got to her first."

"Indeed," Inspector Reed said. "And how do you

know the Hartigans?"

"Old friend of George's," Lord Turnbull said. "Business partners, actually."

"Really?" Ginger said, then lied. "I thought you barely knew each other. I wasn't aware you and my father were in business together?"

"It was long ago, just a small thing. Sadly the business didn't go the way we planned and was soon dissolved."

"So curious," Ginger said lightly. "I'd love to hear more about it."

"Maybe later," Turnbull said, his gaze locking on her glass.

"Oh, yes, please do get yourself a drink," Ginger said.

Lord Turnbull took Ginger up on her offer, and went over to the drinks trolley. Soon after, he held an exotic blue cocktail in one hand as he led Mrs. Fox halfway across the room with the other. Her red evening dress draped seductively over her curves and a crepe skirt bloomed out from her hips. She looked as glamorous as a film star.

"Is that Eunice Hathaway?" Lady Brackenbury shouted. The room went silent and all that was heard was the repeated scratch of a gramophone needle on a record at the end of play.

Finally Lord Brackenbury removed his pipe and spoke. "No dear. That's Lord Turnbull's new gal."

"What?"

"It's Turnbull's new gal!"

Basil Reed whispered into Ginger's ear. "I'm going to surmise that Mrs. Fox and Miss Hathaway resemble each other."

Good old Pippins put on a new record and Bessie Smith's voice filled the dead space.

William Hayes approached. "What is *he* doing here?"

"You don't like Lord Turnbull," Ginger said. "Do you?"

"Nobody likes Lord Turnbull. He's an egomaniac and a bully. If he stays, I'm leaving!"

"Oh, Mr. Hayes," Ginger said, putting a palm to his chest. "You must stay. Mrs. Thornton has cooked a most delicious roast dinner. Surely you won't give up a chance for a home-cooked meal because of one distasteful personality?"

William Hayes' eyes flitted around the room—to Dr. Longden standing alone with a frown on his face—and back to Ginger and the inspector. "You're right. I'm not going to let Turnbull push me around."

Mr. Hayes returned to the drinks trolley, and Dr. Longden stepped forward, Ginger supposed to express his grievances as well.

"I fear you're also not a fan of Lord Turnbull's either?" she said.

The doctor clicked his tongue. "I've known Maxwell Turnbull his whole life. I'm the Turnbull family doctor. Lord and Lady Turnbull doted on him, you see, he was their only child and the only heir. I feared he'd grow up spoiled and entitled and I was right. I tended to his injuries when he was sent home during the war."

"The scar on his forehead?" Basil Reed asked.

"Yes, I removed the stitches."

The doctor scanned the floor in deep thought as if he

wanted to say something else, but was bound by his oath as a doctor.

"Is something wrong?" Ginger said.

The doctor's gaze settled on Harriet Fox. "I'm afraid the woman may be in danger."

Basil looked at him seriously. "Why do you say that?"

"She looks a lot like her. The reddish-blonde hair, a similar figure."

"And she's wearing a very similar dress," Ginger added. She'd noticed the Lucile gown right away.

"Yes," the doctor said. "Now that you mention it."

"Why do you think the young woman might be in danger?" Basil pressed.

"His wife died in suspicious circumstances."

"A fall down the stairs, I believe," Basil said.

"Yes, that's right. And this woman looks so much like the one from ten years … wait a minute, is that what this is about? I read in the paper last week that she was the owner of the remains that were found in the attic here."

"Dr. Longden," Ginger said softly. "Please don't give us away. We're endeavouring to recreate that evening and hopefully get a little closer to bringing Eunice Hathaway some justice."

"Yes. Of course. I would do anything to keep another young life from being tragically cut short."

Ginger checked the time. The Moreaus were late. They might not arrive at all. She clapped her hands calling everyone to attention.

"Please, everyone, dinner is ready. Let's dine together as we remember my father, George Hartigan."

Glasses lifted and a chorus of cheer emitted for Mr. Hartigan.

Pippins led the way to the dining room as their guests followed, with only Bailey remaining behind should anyone require a drink. Lord and Lady Brackenbury shuffled slowly at the rear. Lord Brackenbury leaned into Ginger and whispered, "Watch out for that Turnbull fella."

Ginger and Basil waited until the guests were seated and were about to join them when the doorbell chimed.

"That would be the Moreaus," Ginger said. Since she was near the foyer and Pippins away in the kitchen, she answered it herself.

"Monsieur Moreau!" Ginger said with a perfect French accent. They engaged in the double cheek kiss, a common French greeting. Her smile froze when Monsieur Gaston Moreau introduced his wife.

The woman stared as the bouquet of wild flowers she carried slipped to the floor. "*Mon Dieu*, is that you, Mademoiselle LaFleur?"

Before Ginger could answer, Madame Moreau threw her arms around Ginger and broke into French.

"Antoinette, I thought you were dead! No one would tell me anything. You saved my life! I can't believe it's you!"

Ginger swallowed hard. She remembered Madame Moreau well. During the war she had been known as Mademoiselle Julia Durand. Ginger had run an operation through Julia's family-run hotel. To secure the Durand family's trust, Ginger had forged a friendship with the daughter. It had begun as a mission, but in the end, Ginger had grown close to Julia and had shed many tears over the loss of their friendship when she had to ship away.

"I'm sorry," Ginger said in English. "But you must have me mistaken for someone else."

Julia Moreau jerked back as if she'd just been slapped. "But you look so much … and sound like …"

Ginger forced a laugh. "Goodness gracious, I must have a *doppelgänger*!"

Julia looked close to tears. She grabbed onto her husband. "I feel so silly now."

"Please don't," Ginger said.

Pippins arrived to take their coats. Had he been there long enough to witness Julia's confession? Ginger hoped not.

"Pippins, please collect the blossoms that have fallen to the floor and find a vase."

"Dinner is ready, Monsieur and Madame Moreau," Ginger said brightly. "A good meal is what you need."

Basil Reed led Ginger into the dining room by the elbow and spoke softly into her ear.

"One of these days you're going to explain what just happened."

CHAPTER NINETEEN

THE DINING ROOM TABLE was exquisitely laid out. Fine china, sparkly silverware, crystal vases with garden lilies all glistening under recently dusted electric chandeliers. Ginger made a mental note to give Mrs. Thornton a bonus after this.

Fifteen being an odd number left one person without a corresponding partner, so Ginger had arranged to be seated at the end of the table. She was the hostess of the evening after all.

Basil Reed sat to Ginger's right with Haley, Felicia, Ambrosia, Julia Moreau, Lady Brackenbury and Dr. Longden down the line. To her left was Lord Turnbull with Harriet Fox beside him, then Alfred Schofield, Mrs. Schofield, Gaston Moreau, Lord Brackenbury and William

Hayes.

"Welcome everyone," Ginger said. "Please do enjoy your meal. *Bon appétit!*"

Lizzie and Grace dished out the soup, a delectable lobster bisque, while Pippins poured champagne into the empty flutes.

"Smells divine," Harriet said. "My compliments to the cook."

"We're very fortunate to have Mrs. Thornton come back to us after all these years," Ginger said.

Casual conversation sprung up as the starter was completed and the main course of roast mutton in cream sauce paired with rosemary-covered baked potatoes was brought out.

"I'd like to make a toast," Ginger said to her guests. She lifted her champagne glass. "To my father, a good and dear man, Mr. George Hartigan."

A chorus of *hear, hear*, rang out.

Glasses along the table lifted and champagne was consumed. When Harriet lifted her glass, she flashed a prominent ruby ring on her finger.

"Mrs. Fox, what a fine ring you have," Ginger said.

"Isn't it just beautiful!" Harriet said. "It's a gift from Maxwell."

Before Ginger could respond, a loud crash at the sideboard turned all heads. Mrs. Thornton's face reddened as she curtsied to the table and apologised. "My apologies, Lady Gold. I'm all fingers and thumbs."

Ginger spotted a silver jug on the floor. "It's quite all right, Mrs. Thornton. It's only water."

Lizzie appeared with the mop and the affair was quickly cleaned away.

Harriet caught the inspector's eye. "I don't think we've officially been introduced."

Ginger jumped in. "My apologies. Mrs. Harriet Fox, this is my good friend, Chief Inspector Basil Reed."

"Inspector!" Harriet said. Her eyes darted to Lord Turnbull who'd gone still.

"Everyone must have a profession," Basil Reed said. "But tonight, I'm here as Lady Gold's friend. You must call me Basil."

Harriet's painted lips pulled up into a broad smile. "Then you must call me Harriet."

Ginger wasn't the only one who didn't like this rapid move to intimacy between Basil Reed and a suspect who happened to look like a fashion model.

Lord Turnbull made a show of taking Harriet's hand, the one wearing the ring, and squeezing it. By the way Harriet's eyes pinched together, and her gaze latched onto Maxwell Turnbull, Ginger guessed he was gripping a little too tight.

"It's such tremendous good fortune to see you again, Harriet," Ginger said. Even though the woman's offer of first name usage was extended to Basil Reed, Ginger took the liberty to use it as well.

"Yes, *Ginger*, I remember. In Boston, you were quite the precocious child."

"And you were younger as well."

Harriet Fox frowned but remained silent. No woman liked to be reminded that they had aged.

"Tell me," Ginger continued. "Are you still in contact with my stepmother, Sally?"

Harriet smirked. "It was your *father* I was friends with, not his wife."

Whatever kind of relationship Harriet had had with Ginger's father wasn't something Lord Turnbull approved of. He clutched Harriet's hand tighter.

This time she couldn't help but yelp. "Maxwell!"

"I'm sorry darling," Lord Turnbull said smoothly. He released his hold of her hand, but it wasn't enough to soothe Harriet. She pushed away from the table.

"Where might I find the bathroom?" she said.

Ginger pointed down the hall. "There's one there, first door to your left."

Basil Reed caught Ginger's eye, and she knew what he was thinking. Trouble in paradise already.

"What is it that you do, Lord Turnbull?" Basil Reed asked.

"Oh, a bit of this and a bit of that. It's all just for fun, really. One must do something with one's time." His dark eyes glistened with superiority. "I'm not in *actual* financial need."

"How nice for you," was Basil's simple reply.

Ginger happened to know that Inspector Reed wasn't in actual financial need either. After all, she had met him on the *first-class* deck of the SS *Rosa*. And on further inquiries, discovered that his family line had done well in railways. She was sure Basil would be furious if he knew she'd been snooping about in his past. She'd also confirmed that his marriage was in trouble, which didn't surprise Ginger since

Mrs. Reed had continued to be an absentee for the last two years. She'd filed for divorce, yet the inspector refused to sign the papers.

Basil Reed liked his job at Scotland Yard, and Ginger respected him for pursuing his real interests, even if the pay and social standing didn't align with the status of his family.

"If you'll excuse me, gentlemen," Ginger said. Harriet had been gone a while and Ginger wanted to check up on her. Harriet was just leaving the bathroom when Ginger got there. She had reapplied her makeup, her shadow now darker, her mascara thicker, her lipstick a deeper red. Despite her efforts, Ginger could tell she was upset.

"Is everything okay?" she asked.

"Just dandy. Maxwell is a dear, but sometimes I could just kill him." She forced a grin. "Men, you know?"

Ginger only nodded and made use of the convenience herself.

She found Haley waiting in the hall, arms crossed as she leaned against the wall. "How's our dear Miss Harriet?" Haley asked.

"Tormented, I'm afraid."

"That much is obvious."

"I'm worried about her, Haley. We must make sure she gets home safely tonight. I'd hate for another guest of Lord Turnbull's to go missing after a soirée at Hartigan House."

"Agreed."

By the time they got back to the table, apple pie and whipped cream had been served.

"Darling, you must taste this," Lord Turnbull said

when Harriet pushed her serving aside. He lifted his fork to her and tried to make her smile, but she refused to be cheered. Their tense ongoing silence allowed Ginger to take in snippets of conversation further down the table.

Alfred Schofield: Do you come to London often?

Felicia: Not as nearly as I would like. But now that my sister has moved here …

Alfred Schofield: I could show you about, if you'd like.

Felicia: I'd love that!

Mrs. Schofield: That's an *interesting* brooch Dowager Lady Gold.

Ambrosia: If by interesting you mean old, well it is. Its value to me is sentimental.

Mrs. Schofield: I meant no offence.

Ambrosia: (disbelieving expression of contempt)

Gaston Moreau: Are you enjoying your meal, darling?

Julia Moreau: Oh yes. It's delightful.

Ginger's heart pinched as she watched her old friend, quiet in her own embarrassment—perhaps from joy turned quickly back to grief. Ginger's arms ached with the desire to go to her. If only she could reveal all she'd jump at the chance to comfort Julia. But alas, she was bound by confidentiality. She swallowed a lump and forced herself to look away.

Lord Brackenbury: You've got something on your chin.

Lady Brackenbury: What?

Lord Brackenbury: You've got something on your chin!

Ambrosia: Oh, for heaven's sake.

Dr. Longden: Is something on your mind, Mr. Hayes.

William Hayes: Indeed. I'm feeling a sense of *déjà vu*.

The solicitor's head turned as he sought out Ginger at the head of the table. "I say," he said loudly. "What the deuce is this all about?"

CHAPTER TWENTY

"MY DEAR MAN," Alfred said. "What are you going on about?"

"You weren't here ten years ago Lieutenant Schofield," William Hayes said seriously. "But your grandfather was." He stood dramatically and raised an arm. "Show of hands—who was a guest at Mr. Hartigan's winter soirée of thirteen?"

Slowly the hands went up: Dr. Longden, Gaston Moreau, Mrs. Schofield, Lord and Lady Brackenbury.

Lord Turnbull didn't lift his hand. Instead he jumped to his feet and threw his serviette on his chair. "I demand an explanation."

"Certainly, it's just a coincidence," Ginger said calmly. "Father's friends then remain Father's friends now.

There are just as many here tonight that weren't here that night, including me."

"And don't forget," Mrs. Schofield said importantly, "those who were here then and aren't here tonight, including my dear husband. There was Mr. and Mrs. Hartigan, of course, and poor Eunice Hathaway."

"There you go," Ginger said quickly before conversation about Eunice Hathaway could erupt. "Please now, everyone, enjoy your dessert."

Lord Turnbull and Mr. Hayes shared a piercing stare and then sheepishly sat. Ginger took a small forkful of her pie and moaned with culinary pleasure. "Superb. I do like a nice bite of sweet at the end of a fabulous meal."

Haley engaged Harriet in conversation diverting Lord Turnbull's attention enough that Ginger felt it safe to whisper into Inspector Reed's ear. "Shall we drop the bomb in the drawing room?"

Basil Reed nodded. "I don't think it wise to delay."

Thoughts had turned inward, and an uncomfortable silence descended whilst each rapidly consumed the last course of the meal.

Before any could make an excuse for an early departure, Ginger made the announcement. "I haven't been totally honest with you, my friends. Please let us return to the drawing room for drinks and I'll explain."

Many looks were exchanged, but as Ginger had hoped, she'd snared them with their own curious natures.

Ginger led the way back to the drawing room, bumping into Mrs. Thornton who was just leaving. She seemed shocked to have been caught working and explained quickly. "My apologies, madam. I thought your guests might like some biscuits."

"How thoughtful, Mrs. Thornton." Ginger couldn't imagine taking another bite, but it was quite possible that others might enjoy the comfort something sweet could bring when the bomb fell.

Pippins and Bailey stood ready to serve drinks.

"Where did our Marvin go?" Ginger asked.

"I sent him to help in the kitchen, madam," Pippins said.

"Good idea. I'm sure Mrs. Thornton would appreciate the extra help."

Pippins and Bailey mixed and poured drinks, giving Ginger her request for the night of scotch and soda, mostly soda, and the inspector his rum cola, mostly cola. She was impressed with how they had memorised everyone's preferences including another Blue Marlin—a rum cocktail with blue Curacao and lime juice—for Lord Turnbull, which was probably the easiest to remember of all.

They assembled themselves in a semicircle: the women sitting and the men standing.

"Please get on with it," Lord Turnbull said after a long sip. "Why are we really here?"

Basil Reed stepped forward. "As you may or may not know, I'm a chief inspector of the Criminal Investigation Department at Scotland Yard." His pronouncement elicited light gasps from those who had in fact not known.

He continued, "Though Lady Gold was earnest in her desire to gather friends to honour the late Mr. Hartigan, there is another underlying motive. And that is to gather those who were present on the night Miss Eunice Hathaway went missing. So your assumption in the dining room, Mr. Hayes, was correct. As you are likely aware, this is now a murder investigation. Miss Hathaway's body has been found."

Low murmurs all around expressed dismay at their hostess's deceit. Lady Brackenbury was completely lost at sea. She yelled out, "What?"

Lord Brackenbury shouted in her ear, "I'll tell you all about it at home." He passed her one of the plates with Mrs. Thornton's biscuits, and she accepted it in conciliation.

"Well, now that it's all in the open," Mrs. Schofield said, "I should love to hear how her body ended up in the attic of Hartigan House."

Ambrosia's hand went to her chest in dismay. "Mrs. Schofield!"

"I'm simply stating the facts," Mrs. Schofield said, unruffled.

"We'll get to all that in good time," Basil Reed said.

"I dare say," Lord Turnbull said. His voice had developed a lisp, and he swayed slightly as he swung his near-empty glass about. Ginger frowned. Just how strong had Pippins made his drink?

"I dare say," Lord Turnbull repeated. "This is th-lighly underhand-ed."

Basil Reed cast a glance at Ginger before answering. "We apologise. It was thought the easiest way to get you together in order to ask questions—officially, I might add. You were served a nice meal for your trouble."

"Then do get on with it," Lord Brackenbury said with annoyance. "I'll be up half the night relating this to my wife."

"Indeed," Basil said. "Lord Brackenbury, let's begin with you. Do you recall engaging in conversation with Miss Hathaway on the night of the thirty-first of December 1913, or recall overhearing your wife doing the same?"

"I do not. She was much younger than either of us, even back then. The type of youth who considered the elderly as they would consider the furniture. Useful, but not necessary."

"You didn't care for Miss Hathaway, I take it?"

"I didn't say that. I didn't know her well enough to make a judgment. Lady Brackenbury and I spent most of the time talking to Mr. and Mrs. Schofield."

"That's right," Mrs. Schofield said. "Mr. Schofield and I had a conversation on the way home about how pleasant the Brackenburys were and how we might meet up with them again. Unfortunately, my Albert passed away not long afterwards, and Lady Brackenbury ... well, she took a turn for the worse."

Lady Brackenbury obviously could hear well enough to make out her name. She let out a spittle of crumbs with a boisterous, "What?"

Felicia let out a bout of laughter then clapped her hand over her mouth. "I do apologise. This is all just so jolly-well entertaining!"

"Do get a hold of yourself, child," Ambrosia snapped. "This is a serious matter." To the room she added. "Youth these days! They have no idea how to take anything seriously. Life is all fun and games for them."

Haley, who was seated next to Ginger, whispered, "I think the Gold women have had enough to drink. Present company excepted."

Ginger nodded. "Not everyone knows how to hold their liquor."

Basil Reed cleared his throat. "Yes, right. Does anyone else recall conversing with Miss Hathaway that night?"

"I spoke to her," Dr. Longden said. "She was complaining of a headache and asked if I had an aspirin."

"Did you give her an aspirin, Dr. Longden?" Basil Reed asked.

"Why yes, I did. But ... you don't think I ..."

"I'm not accusing anyone, Doctor," Basil said. "Anyone else?"

"I only conversed with her in the presence of Lord Turnbull," William Hayes said. "I believe we spoke about the inclement weather."

Mrs. Schofield scoffed. "The weather my foot. I saw the three of you huddled in intense conversation. Ask Lord Turnbull."

Lord Turnbull stared at her with glassy eyes. Mr. Hayes filled the silence. "I didn't like the way Turnbull was treating the young woman. I simply offered to represent her, should she want to file a complaint. Turnbull, in turn, threatened my life."

Ginger didn't miss how Mr. Hayes refused to use Maxwell Turnbull's title.

"Bill," Lord Turnbull said as if his tongue had

thickened. "Can I call you Bill?" He toppled a bit. "You're *th*uch a little weasel of a man."

William Hayes seethed. "And you're a drunk, Turnbull!" He shook a fist. "You're going to be sorry for this."

Ginger quickly rose to her feet. "Now, now, gentlemen. Let's be civil, shall we?"

Basil Reed nodded at Ginger and she slowly reclaimed her seat. "Anyone else?" he said.

Mrs. Schofield sat upright. "We talked at length about her gorgeous ring," she offered. "I quite admired it. A lovely ruby. Much like the one Mrs. Fox is wearing, I might say."

All eyes turned to Harriet Fox. She casually sipped on her champagne, blatantly displaying the jewel to all.

"Eunice!" Lord Turnbull shouted, breaking the silence that had filled the room. He stumbled across the drawing room like a drunkard. "Is that you?" He fell to the floor at Harriet's feet, pulling at her dress in a most ungentlemanly manner. "Eunice!"

Harriet stared at the man with abhorrence. "Maxwell! Get off me!"

"I'm sorry … Bailey …"

Lord Turnbull collapsed to the floor.

Eyes shifted to Bailey who shrugged his shoulders, and back to the man on the floor. Bailey, who seemed to come to his senses, rushed to his employer's side, getting there right behind Ginger, Basil and Dr. Longden.

The doctor checked for a pulse, then shook his head. "He's dead."

Lee Strauss

CHAPTER TWENTY-ONE

A REFRAIN OF "my good Lord!" and "not dead, surely," erupted.

Mrs. Schofield remained level-headed with her cool response of, "Well, this is unexpected."

Ambrosia slumped in her chair in a faint with Felicia hovering over her, "Grandmama! Wake up!"

Lady Brackenbury's neck turned rapidly as she tried to decipher the uproar, all the while yelling, "What? What?" Lord Brackenbury shouted in return. "Turnbull's dead!"

The Moreaus spoke rapidly to each other in French. "*Est-il vraiment mort?*"

Haley worked the room trying to get everyone to calm down. "Keep your heads, everyone!"

Inspector Reed huddled with Dr. Longden. Ginger stood close enough to listen in.

"It could be a heart attack," Dr. Longden said, "though he's still fairly young and appears to be fit."

"Or poison?" Ginger said, nudging her way into the huddle. "Isn't that a rash on his neck?"

"To be sure, poison is a possibility," the doctor said solemnly. "However, we'll know more after an autopsy's been done. I'd be happy to perform it."

"Thank you, Doctor," Basil Reed said. "But we'll need to ask someone who's not personally connected to the case to do it."

"I see," the doctor said. "I'm connected because I'm one of the guests here."

"Precisely."

Alfred Schofield approached Ginger. "I'm going to take grandmother home. This event is proving too upsetting for her." Ginger did a quick inventory and concluded that Mrs. Schofield seemed to be the least emotional of all the women that were close to her age. Felicia was still calming a nervous Ambrosia, and Lord Brackenbury was singing loudly into Lady Brackenbury's ear.

"I'm sorry, but I can't allow you to leave," Inspector Reed said. He turned to the room. "Can I have everyone's attention?"

The guests calmed and listened attentively.

"No one is to leave Hartigan House until I say."

The silence once again was shattered with everybody speaking at once.

William Hayes: "You can't hold us hostage."

Alfred Schofield: "It's late. Surely you must let the older ladies go ..."

Harriet Fox: "Are we prisoners now?"

Andrew Bailey: "What have we to do with Lord Turnbull's demise?"

Lady Brackenbury: "What?"

Inspector Reed put two fingers in his mouth and whistled loudly. The room stilled.

"Until I give the okay, no one leaves—that includes all guests, staff, and occupants of Hartigan House. And please, do not touch anything!"

A low disgruntled murmur resumed.

Turning to Ginger, Basil Reed said, "I believe it would be best if we gathered everyone into the sitting room."

"Certainly."

Basil gave instructions, and he and Ginger watched as her guests filed after Pippins as if he were the Pied Piper.

Once the drawing room was emptied of all—except poor Lord Turnbull—Ginger closed and locked the door.

"Might I use your telephone?" Basil asked.

"Of course. You know where it is."

"Please, watch that no one leaves the sitting room."

Haley positioned herself with Ginger who stood in the arched entranceway to the sitting room, preventing access to the front door.

The fresher air from the foyer awakened Ginger's nose to the unpleasant odour that had attached itself to the group: a mix of cigar and cigarette smoke, heavy perfume, and nervous sweat. Haley noticing it as well, wrinkled her nose. "What a fine-looking, smelly bunch we are."

"Indeed," Ginger said, keeping her voice low. "What do you think caused Lord Turnbull to die so suddenly like that?"

"I don't think it was a heart attack," Haley said. "If you remember, his speech had slurred before he fell and I noticed him having a faraway look."

"You don't think he was simply inebriated?"

"Lord Turnbull didn't appear to be a man who couldn't hold his liquor. He put quite a few glasses of champagne away over dinner and never stumbled with his speech once."

Ginger turned to Haley with searching eyes. "You think he was poisoned."

"I think it's more than likely he was poisoned, but I wouldn't swear to it before a post-mortem has been performed."

Ginger folded her arms over her chest. "I wonder what the poison was—if it was indeed poisoning." Her gaze scanned the drawing room. Except Pippins and Basil Reed, everyone was accounted for: Mrs. and Alfred Schofield, Lord and Lady Brackenbury, Ambrosia and Felicia, Harriet Fox, Andrew Bailey, the Moreaus, Dr. Longden, and William Hayes.

She sang softly to herself, "I wonder who the killer is?"

People dealt with stress in different ways. Some liked to close their eyes and doze off, like Lady Brackenbury and Ambrosia: some stared into space with a faraway look, such as Harriet Fox and Felicia. Others, simply put out, constantly checked their watches, like Dr. Longden and Mrs. Schofield. Then there were those who got agitated, shifting their weight from foot to foot, clenching and unclenching their fists, continuously running palms over well-oiled hair or fussing with their ties, like Alfred Schofield and William Hayes. The latter to the point of showing uncharacteristic behaviour for one in his profession. He strolled swiftly towards the doorway, exclaiming, "Lady Gold, you have no legal right to hold us here. Lord Turnbull has obviously suffered a stroke or heart attack."

Haley stepped forward. "Mr. Hayes, you will step back and cooperate with the police."

William Hayes pushed her aside and made a run for the foyer.

"Stop right there!" Ginger had wondered if the small Remington derringer she'd tucked into her garter would come into play before the evening was out. She pointed it at William Hayes, pushing the hammer down with a menacing click. A loud gasp escaped the lips of the onlookers. Ginger stood straight, legs spread, her dress tight against her knees, elbows locked, and gun pointed.

"It's been a while since I've used this thing, Mr. Hayes," she said, staring him straight in the eye. "But I haven't forgotten how."

CHAPTER TWENTY-TWO

INSPECTOR REED returned, his eyes wide with speculation as he took in Ginger's stance with the gun. William Hayes made a quick retreat back to his position in the sitting room and Ginger relaxed her hold.

"Just doing my job, Inspector," she said with a smile. She lifted the hem of her dress until it reached her garter and slipped the weapon back into place.

Inspector Reed froze as he watched her, shook his head and cleared his throat. He stepped around her into the sitting room, with the whole of Ginger's staff behind him. Pippins, Mrs. Thornton, Lizzie, Grace, Marvin and Scout.

"Hold up there, young man," Ginger said, pulling Scout back before he could get wind of the tragedy. She winked at him. "You can wait here with me."

"Aw, can't I see the body, missus?"

"Certainly not!" It seemed he'd already heard. How quickly bad news travels amongst the ranks. Scout smiled his toothy grin and her heart ached to protect his innocence. The lad had seen so much hardship already in his young life: she wouldn't expose him to this as well. She waved Felicia over.

"Felicia, would you mind taking young Scout to the kitchen?"

Felicia glanced back at Ambrosia whose head was pressed against the wing of the chair. Her chin tilted up, her mouth open, and her eyes closed. A soft snore was heard as she exhaled.

"I'd be happy to," Felicia said. "I think Grandmama is quite knackered at the moment." She knelt to the boy's level. "Do you like biscuits?"

Scout nodded shyly. "Uh-huh."

"Great. Let's go and see if we can find some!" Felicia took Scout's hand and they disappeared down the hall to the kitchen.

Ginger turned her attention back to the drama going on in the sitting room.

Inspector Reed announced to the room, "The police are on their way, at which time I shall see you one by one and you shall make a statement. After that, you will be free to go.

To Ginger, he added, "May I use your study to conduct the interviews?"

"Of course, Inspector."

Ten minutes later Pippins showed Sergeant Scott and Constable Newman into the room.

Basil nodded to the men and got right to the point. "Newman, I need you to watch this room, ensure that no one leaves until released by me. Scott please take the drawing room and watch the body. Make sure no one but the forensics team, and persons I authorize, enter."

Pippins left with Sergeant Scott to unlock the drawing room door.

Basil Reed consulted his pocket-sized notebook. "Lord Brackenbury, I'll see you first."

"Haley?" Ginger said quietly. "Would you mind distracting Lady Brackenbury until his lordship has finished?"

"I'd be happy to."

Ginger led Inspector Reed and Lord Brackenbury down the dimly lit passage to the study at the back of the house. The room had French windows that opened out to the garden terrace, not easily seen in the darkness of night.

"Help yourself to my father's chair," Ginger said to Basil Reed. "My chair now," she amended.

Two leather chairs faced the desk. Lord Brackenbury sat in one; Ginger claimed the other.

Inspector Reed stared at her. "Lady Gold, I'm accustomed to doing the interviews on my own."

"Are you really? It's my understanding that there are always two in the room—for proper documentation and such—, and since your two officers are currently needed elsewhere, allow me to be of assistance." Ginger picked up a pad of paper and fountain pen from the desktop. "I'm ready to take notes."

Basil Reed sighed and conceded. "Very well. But I'll hold you to the strictest confidence, Lady Gold."

"As God is my witness," she said.

Straightening his tie, Inspector Reed began, "Lord Brackenbury, let's be swift so you can take your wife home. I'm certain you're both fatigued."

The elderly man nodded. "We are."

"What is your relationship with the deceased?"

"I have no relationship. I only encountered the man at occasional social affairs where we had acquaintances in common."

"Have you ever been in a business relationship with Lord Turnbull?"

"I have not."

"Can you recall the night of the thirty-first of December 1913?"

"I can. Unlike my poor wife, my mind is as sharp now as it was then."

"Brilliant. Then you'll remember Eunice Hathaway. What are your thoughts about her on that night?"

"Miss Hathaway was a young, flighty thing, acting the part, but not at all suited for it."

"The part?" Ginger asked. Basil Reed shot her a look. She ignored it.

"She acted as if she knew the ways of the upper class, like she was one of us. She most definitely was not."

"It's my understanding the Hathaways are quite well off," Ginger said.

"Well, yes," Lord Brackenbury said. "It's well known

they made their fortune in African gold. New money, you see. And ..." He leaned forward and lowered his voice, "I'm not one for gossip, mind you, but word does get about. Miss Eunice was adopted. It was believed she was the love child of Mr. Hathaway and that Mrs. Hathaway agreed to take her in to avoid a scandal."

"Really?" Ginger said. "She and Miss Hathaway must've had an interesting mother-daughter relationship."

"It was quite in name only," Lord Brackenbury said. "If you can trust what you hear. Miss Hathaway didn't do much in the way of bringing respectability to the family name or to the reputation of the upper class, truth be told."

"Do you believe Miss Hathaway got what she deserved?" the inspector asked.

Lord Brackenbury jerked back with a look of shock on his face. "I most certainly do not! No one deserves to be *murdered.* The end of our days on earth should be up to God and God alone."

"That will be all, Lord Brackenbury. Thank you for your time. You may take Lady Brackenbury home."

"Thank you, Inspector."

Ginger waited until the older man had disappeared and was out of earshot.

"That was interesting," she said.

"Indeed, if in fact there is any truth to the rumours. Now, would you mind calling the young lads in?" Basil Reed's gaze fell to his notes. "Marvin and Scout Elliot."

Ginger inclined her head. "Am I your secretary now?"

"You are if you want to stay in this room."

Ginger jumped from her chair. "Understood."

Moments later the Elliot boys were in the chairs in front of the desk. Ginger leaned against the bookshelf, notebook in hand. Marvin and Scout sat stiffly before the inspector, frightened expressions on their youthful faces. Scout's skinny legs dangled, his feet not quite touching the floor.

"It's all right, boys," Ginger said gently. She expected that both Marvin and Scout had things they'd rather the chief inspector didn't find out about. "You're not in trouble. Inspector Reed just has a few quick questions about tonight's event."

"All right, madam," Marvin said. "Sir."

"Mr. Elliot," Inspector Reed began."

Marvin and Scout said together, "Uh-huh?"

Basil and Ginger exchanged amused glances. Basil tried again.

"How about I call the eldest Mr. Elliot, Mr. Elliot, and the younger one, Mr. Scout?"

The boys nodded and Marvin answered, "Righto, sir."

"Mr. Elliot, you assisted Mr. Pippins and Mr. Bailey with the drinks, is that so?"

"Yes, sir. Until the supper. Den I was in the kitchen wiv Scout."

"While you were serving the drinks, did you see anything suspicious? Someone tampering with one of the bottles, say, or someone behind the drinks trolley who shouldn't have been there?"

Marvin worked the muscles in his face as if that

would help him in remembering. "No, sir. I dinnit see nuthin' like dat."

"Mr. Elliot, have you come in contact with any of tonight's guests outside of this evening, either socially or otherwise?"

Marvin and Scout shared a look. Marvin worked his lips.

"No, sir."

"Marvin, darling," Ginger said. "You can tell the inspector the truth. We know you didn't do anything to Lord Turnbull."

Basil nodded and smiled. "That's true. I just want to solve this crime—if it is a crime—and you never know what little thing might break the case."

Marvin scratched the back of his neck. "I seen the lady in the red dress, down by the docks. She has no business there unless it's bad business."

Ginger couldn't guess what Harriet Fox would be doing by the docks, but it didn't speak highly of her character.

"Wat about me?" Scout swung his legs excitedly. "Ya gonna ask me some questions, sir?"

Ginger held in a laugh and saw that Basil was doing the same.

"I am indeed, Mr. Scout. Now let's see…"

"I saw the lady in the red dress too, outsida the solicitor's office. Saw dat solicitor come to fisticuffs wiv the dead guy. Right, missus?" He looked to Ginger.

Scout's eager expression looked to Ginger for validation. It could be assumed that most adults, especially on this side of London, wouldn't believe him.

"Lady Gold," Basil said, the humour in his eyes disappearing. "Why is this lad looking to you?"

Scout looked stricken. "Sorry, missus. I shoulda kept me mouf shut."

"It's all right, Scout."

Ginger straightened her shoulders. "If you recall, Inspector Reed, young Scout and I became acquainted on the SS *Rosa*. He helped me ... with my investigation."

"*That* was *my* investigation." Basil Reed's eyes narrowed as a memory returned. "*He* was your *witness*?"

Ginger folded her arms across her chest and looked down her nose. "I will not answer that. I will not give away the names of my confidential informers."

Basil threw his pen on the desktop in a huff. "Unbelievable."

"Have you finished with these fine young men?" Ginger said stiffly. "I'm sure they're tired out."

"Yes, all right. Mr. Elliot, Mr. Scout, you may go."

Ginger ushered the boys out, found Pippins and told him to call them a taxicab. She then returned to the study. It was enough time for Basil to gain his composure. She slid into one of the chairs, crossed her legs and folded her arms.

Basil stared at her with disbelief. "Don't tell me you're using kids to do your dirty work."

"I simply want to give the boys money, a few bob to take the pinch off, but they're too proud to take it unless I attach a little job to it."

Basil considered her point. "I have to respect them for that."

"Well, so do I. I'd never ask them to do anything that would put them in danger, and I'm quite offended that you would assume that I would."

"I'm sorry, you're right." Basil suddenly looked fatigued. "My job has trained me to look for the worst in people. You've given me no reason to doubt your character."

Ginger smiled, reached across the desk and gripped the inspector's hand. "You're forgiven."

They stared at their joined hands, then at each other before Ginger slowly pulled her hand away and laid it on her lap.

"Lady Gold ..."

Ginger held a palm up. "Ginger. We agreed to use our Christian names."

Basil Reed relaxed in his chair. His hazel eyes settled on Ginger in a way that made her stomach tingle, and his mouth pulled up into a crooked grin. "You're right, though strictly speaking, I believe Ginger is a nickname."

Ginger shrugged. "You can call me Georgia if you like."

"You obviously prefer Ginger, so I'll stick to that."

Ginger stood and stuck her hip out defiantly. "You said you thought it was cute."

The inspector's grin grew wider. "And it is." He cleared his throat then referred to his notebook. "*Ginger,* please call in ... "

A knock on the door interrupted them. Haley poked her head into the study. "Sorry to bother you, but I thought you'd like to know that the forensics team is here."

CHAPTER TWENTY-THREE

GINGER AND BASIL headed for the drawing room with Haley. Ginger looked at her friend and said quietly, "How are the troops?"

"The shock seems to have worn off. They're now demonstrating a high level of irritability. *Your class* doesn't take kindly to being inconvenienced, even when one of them dies in their midst."

"I make no excuses," Ginger said.

They approached the forensics team. A tall middle-aged man was busy taking pictures, as another stockier fellow measured distances between the corpse and points in the room to document exact positioning. A thick-shouldered man with a bushy mop of white hair squatted next to the body. He opened Lord Turnbull's shirt and inspected his neck and chest area. The moment he noticed Basil Reed hovering he stood. Knees cracking, he propped himself up with a large hand.

"Hello, Inspector," he said. "I do apologise for taking an age to get here. The night's been active, and I'm short of personnel."

Haley had filled Ginger in on facts of the financial constraints and manpower limitations the London City forensics unit experienced.

"It's good to see you again, Dr. Watts," Basil said.

This was Dr. Watts, Basil's preferred pathologist? Ginger took closer stock. Alan Watts wasn't what you'd call attractive, but he had a genuine air about him, a face you could trust. Ginger pegged him to be in his late fifties, though his white hair made him appear older.

Ginger stretched out her hand. "I'm Ginger Gold. This is my home."

"Lady Gold," Basil corrected.

Dr. Watts's handshake was firm. "Nice to meet you Lady Gold. I've heard a lot about you from Miss Higgins. She's one of my best students."

"All good, I hope," Ginger said with a smile.

"Well," Haley said dryly. "Mostly."

Dr. Watts chuckled. "You have a good friend in Miss Higgins, madam."

"Dr. Watts," Basil Reed began. "I'd like to request fingerprints be obtained from Lord Turnbull's glass, along with the bottles of rum, blue Curacao and lime juice used to make Lord Turnbull's Blue Marlin."

"My butler, Pippins, will advise," Ginger said. "I'll retrieve him." Before she made it to the sitting room, the telephone rang. The call was for Sergeant Scott. Ginger returned shortly with Pippins in tow. As he pointed out the bottles in question, Sergeant Scott rushed into the room.

"The station just called. There's a burglary in process, sir, just a few streets away. Are Newman and I still needed here?"

"I think we now have the cooperation of the crew. Please, go and catch a burglar."

Ginger went to the sitting room and called for Pippins. She removed the revolver from her garter and handed it to him. "Now that the police have gone, I trust you'll guard the door."

Pippins slid the weapon into his pocket. "Yes, madam."

Dr. Watts was behind the drinks trolley with his dusting kit open when Ginger returned to the drawing room. "Lord Turnbull had an interesting taste in cocktails," he said. "The blue colour of the Curacao would conceal a foreign substance added to it, and the rum would mask any bitterness in taste."

"So you believe it was poison and not a heart attack?" Basil Reed said. "He did grab at his chest as he fell to the ground."

"Many poisons work by constricting blood flow to the heart. The accompanying rash on his chest makes me believe it was poison, though I won't make an official statement until the post-mortem is completed."

"How long before that's done?" Inspector Reed asked.

Dr. Watts paused from his work. "There's an unfortunate backlog in all the labs in the city. Must be a full moon. Lord Turnbull shall be sent to my lab. I should get it done in a day or two." He glanced at Haley. "If Miss Higgins agrees to assist, it might go quicker."

Haley snorted. "Horses couldn't hold me back, Doctor."

Haley remained behind with the forensics team as Ginger and Basil returned to the sitting room. Haley's assessment of the mood there proved to be true. The inspector was pounced upon the minute he stepped foot across the threshold.

Surely, he had no reason to hold them against their will!
Your superintendent shall be hearing from me!

"Calm down and make way!" Basil Reed knew how to wield his authority, and everyone stepped back. "We'll take statements as quickly as possible." He referred to his watch. "I aim to have you all out of here by midnight. Mrs. Fox, I'll see you next.

Harriet Fox rose gracefully, keeping expert command of her expression. Nothing was written there—not grief, nor remorse nor guilt. Mrs. Fox's eyes were a disconcerting icy blue, and Ginger had to wonder if her heart was as cold as her eyes.

Ginger took the seat beside Harriet Fox as Basil reclaimed her father's chair.

"Do you mind if I smoke?" Harriet asked.

Basil cast a glance at Ginger, who nodded consent.

"Go ahead," he said.

Harriet snapped open her small handbag, removed an ivory holder and gold-plated cigarette case. A gift from Lord Turnbull? Ginger and Basil were held captive as she methodically inserted a cigarette into the holder and lit it with a silver lighter. She'd recently reapplied her lipstick and left an imprint on the holder when she pulled it out of her mouth to exhale.

Harriet kept her alluring blue eyes on the inspector. "Why is *she* here?"

"To take notes," Basil replied. "Now I promised this would be quick, so let's get started."

Harriet crossed her legs seductively. "Fire away."

Basil's gaze rested on Harriet's calf for a second too long, a fact noticed by both Harriet and Ginger. Ginger cleared her throat.

"Yes," Basil said, recovering his professionalism in time. "Mrs. Fox, how long have you known Lord Turnbull?"

"Ages, darling. We travel in the same circle."

"By ages, do you mean one year? Five years? More than five?"

"Golly, it's hard to pinpoint it. Around five, I'd say."

"How would you describe your relationship to him now?"

"Now? Why Inspector, I'd say it's dead."

Basil frowned. "Let me rephrase. How would you describe your relationship to Lord Turnbull yesterday?"

Harriet blew smoke out of the side of her mouth toward Ginger who flapped the smoke away with her hand.

"My apologies, darling," Harriet said without sparing her a glance.

Basil pressed. "Mrs. Fox?"

"Yes. I'd say our relationship was complicated."

"Can you explain?"

"That's the definition of complicated, isn't it? Difficult to explain?"

"Were you and Lord Turnbull involved?" Ginger asked impatiently. "Physically?"

"Ah. Now we've got to the point, haven't we? Yes, I'll admit to that, at least up until the last couple of months. Lately, well, I was losing interest, you could say."

"And how did Lord Turnbull take the fact that you were losing interest?" Basil asked.

"Not well, darling."

"He seemed to be quite possessive of you tonight," Ginger said. "Was that problematic?"

"No woman likes to be *owned*, Lady Gold. Maxwell could be obnoxious and controlling, especially when he felt like he was losing control."

"Mrs. Fox," Ginger continued. "You stated to me this evening that Lord Turnbull angered you so much you could *kill* him."

"Ah, yes. In retrospect, a poor choice of words." Harriet brought the cigarette to her lips, inhaled, then exhaled with enough force to send the smoke into Ginger's face. "Yes, he angered me, but I didn't kill him. Am I sorry he's dead? Not really. But it wasn't me that killed him."

"Do you know who it was that killed him?" Basil asked.

Harriet chuckled. "That would be too easy, wouldn't it, Inspector. Maxwell had more than a few enemies. Who's to say who it was who finally got to him."

"Someone present this evening," Ginger said.

Harriet blew out a last puff of smoke from her nostrils and then extinguished the cigarette in a compact ashtray she carried. "Well, yes," she said. "I suppose you're right. But it wasn't me."

"You may go, Mrs. Fox," Basil said. "But don't leave town."

Harriet arched a well-shaped brow. "I look forward to being interviewed by you again, Inspector. Perhaps next time we can leave your ... *secretary* behind."

Ginger fumed as Harriet Fox sashayed out of the room.

"You don't like her?" Basil said.

"She's a troublemaker. I'd watch out for her if I were you, and I don't mean like *that*."

"I certainly don't know what you're insinuating, Lady Gold," Basil said, but the twinkle in his eye said the opposite.

He straightened his tie and referred to his notes. "Please ask the Moreaus in."

"I think I need a bit of a break," Ginger said. "Do you mind if I ask Haley to sit in with this interview?"

Basil studied her before replying. "Does this have something to do with the scene earlier, when Madame Moreau mistook you for someone else?"

Ginger scoffed. "No, of course not. I need to visit the lavatory."

"Very well."

Basil was correct in his assumptions. Ginger couldn't face being in a small room with her old friend. It was too intimate. Too dangerous. Too easy to let some small detail slip and confirm to Julia Moreau that her first impulse had been correct.

As Ginger expected, the Moreau interview went quickly and she sighed with relief when they were well on their way.

"By the way," Haley said when Ginger returned to replace her. "Dr. Watts and the team have completed their investigation and have taken the body to the morgue at the university. Dr. Watts asked me to say his goodbyes."

"Thank you, Miss Higgins," Basil said.

The interview with Dr. Longden was uneventful, but Felicia brought interesting information to light.

She looked wretched as she sat in the chair next to her grandmother. "I don't want to get anyone in trouble."

"If you know something you think might help Inspector Reed with his investigation, darling," Ginger said firmly, "it's your duty to relay it."

"Oh bother. It's Lieutenant Schofield. Over dinner he regaled me with tales of his exploits in the war. He flew a Sopwith Camel, you know. They're such frightfully exciting machines. I've seen one at the airfield in Hertfordshire." She let out the sigh of a girl soft on a fella who was out of reach.

"I'm aware of his service to King and country, Miss Gold," Basil said.

"Yes, right. Well, Lieutenant Schofield showed me a

locket he wore around his neck. He said he kept his cyanide capsule there, in case the Germans captured him, and he had to take his life. I thought it so brave and romantic, but now ..." Felicia's expression collapsed in her distress.

"He's not right for you, child," Ambrosia said. "I knew there was something fishy about him the minute I met him. Too big for his boots, I say. All air force men are. They think they're above the rest of us."

Ginger caught Basil's eye and smirked at the unintentional pun.

"Miss Gold," Basil said, "the cause of death hasn't yet been determined. There's no need to jump to any conclusions." He excused the women. Ginger, her arm around Felicia, walked out with them. Basil strolled back to the sitting room and was immediately accosted by Alfred Schofield.

"Inspector! I insist that you call us next. My grandmother—"

"Oh, stop fussing over me, Alfred." Mrs. Schofield grinned at Basil and Ginger. "I'm quite enjoying myself."

Ginger didn't doubt what the woman said in the least. Mrs. Schofield had hit a gold mine of gossip fodder.

"You may come with me now, Mrs. Schofield, Lieutenant Schofield," Basil said. "Except for the staff we're nearly done."

Left standing by the fireplace, William Hayes had his head bowed. His shoulders slumped like the school boy chosen last for cricket. Ginger felt a tad sorry for him.

"Lieutenant Schofield," Basil said once the Schofields

were seated. "Might I see the locket you are wearing around your neck?"

Alfred chuckled. "I knew the yarn I told Miss Gold would come to bite me in the derriere. Had I known Turnbull was going to kick the bucket, I wouldn't have mentioned it."

Basil persisted. "May I see it?"

Alfred relieved himself of a long silver chain with a small square locket and handed it to the inspector.

Basil opened the trinket. "It's empty."

"Of course it is, old chap. Do you think I walk around with a cyanide pill on me?"

"Perhaps if you thought you might have use of it."

"I know what you're thinking. I didn't kill Turnbull."

"That's Lord Turnbull," Basil said. He handed the locket back. "Why wear this at all? The war is over."

Alfred grinned. "Honestly? It impresses the ladies. A great conversation starter if you know what I mean."

"Alfred!" Mrs. Schofield scolded.

"How do you know Lord Turnbull?"

"Only by reputation. It's well-known that he's a pompous ass."

"Alfred!"

"Sorry, Grandmother."

There was a quiet exchange of looks before Alfred began again. "Look here, I know this looks bad, but I'm not your man."

Basil released Alfred who hurried to shuffle a reluctant Mrs. Schofield out the door.

"Mr. Hayes, you are next," Ginger said.

William Hayes heaved a long sigh as he settled into the chair opposite the inspector.

"I do apologise for my behaviour earlier," he said. "It's a knee-jerk response from my boyhood days—fight or flight, you see. Obviously, in stressful situations, I tend to flee. There's a reason why I don't do criminal law."

"I see," said Basil. "How well did you know Lord Turnbull?"

William Hayes reddened as he shifted in his seat. "If you mean socially? Not well at all. In fact I avoided the man at all costs. Had I known he'd be here tonight …"

"We have a witness who says they saw you go to fists in the street."

The blush on William Hayes face spread down his neck.

"That unfortunate scene was the result of a professional encounter."

"Is that so?"

"Yes. And that makes the details of our, uh, disagreement, privileged."

"Hiding behind privilege makes you look guilty, Mr. Hayes," Basil said.

"I may be guilty of many things, Inspector, but I didn't kill Turnbull."

The phrase was starting to sound like a skipping record. The solicitor shifted, crossed his legs, shifted again, and crossed the opposite leg. His overt agitation made Ginger squirm. She couldn't put her finger on why exactly, but she didn't trust this little man.

"My father left his previous solicitor in 1913 to hire

you, Mr. Hayes," she stated.

"Yes. I believe we spoke about this before. That's usually the way things work in law. Solicitors retire. Or one becomes unsatisfied with one's solicitor and moves on to the next."

"Why you?"

William Hayes swallowed and shifted his gaze to anyplace but Ginger's face. *He's hiding something.* Ginger wouldn't stop digging until she knew what.

The solicitor deflected. "Why not me?"

A rapid knock on the door interrupted the interview. Pippins blew in uninvited. Ginger frowned. This behaviour was so unlike her butler.

"What is it Pippins?"

"It's Bailey. He's gone."

CHAPTER TWENTY-FOUR

GINGER AND BASIL jumped to their feet and rushed to the sitting room.

"How long has he been gone?" Ginger asked.

"I'm afraid I can't say, madam," Pippins said. "I only noticed once Mr. Hayes left, and only the staff remained. It suddenly occurred to me that I hadn't seen Bailey in the crowd for some time."

The sitting room felt empty with just the four members of Ginger's household staff plus Mr. Hayes remaining.

"Did anyone see Mr. Bailey leave the room?" she asked.

Lizzie and Grace lowered their gazes to the floor and shook their heads. "No, your ladyship."

"Mrs. Thornton?"

"I've been sittin' in this chair with my feet up. They're killin' me! I'm afraid I dozed off a time or two."

Ginger spoke softly to Basil. "As you know, Andrew Bailey once lived in this house. He'd be attuned to all the ways to get in and out unseen."

"I see. I'll make use of your telephone once more, if I may."

William Hayes stood behind them, wringing his hands. "If you've finished with me … "

"For now," Basil said. "Don't leave town."

William Hayes practically sprinted from the room. He really did tend to flee, Ginger thought as she flopped into an empty chair. Haley sat on the settee.

"This wasn't how I'd imagine this evening would go," Ginger said.

Lizzie approached and bobbed. "Would you and Miss Higgins like some tea, madam?"

"Thank you, Lizzie," Ginger said. "That would be lovely."

Basil Reed returned with his overcoat and his hat in hand.

"Inspector?" Ginger said.

"I've called the Yard. A search is now underway for Mr. Bailey." His eyes scanned Ginger's staff. "Where's Miss Weaver?"

"She's in the kitchen preparing tea. Would you like a cup?"

"No, thank you. It's late. If you don't mind, I'll return tomorrow to question your staff."

"I'm sure they would be more than happy to oblige."

"Good. I'll find my way out. Good night Lady Gold, Miss Higgins."

Lizzie brought in the tea tray and set it on the small table between Ginger and Haley.

"You can all retire for the evening," Ginger told her staff. "I'm sure you all must be simply exhausted. Pippins, do first make sure the house is secure."

"Of course, madam."

Ginger unbuckled her shoes and stretched her feet out on the ottoman. "What a day!" She sipped on her cup of tea and stared at the simmering embers in the fireplace.

"I prefer a quiet house," Haley said, tea in hand.

"How's the tea?" Ginger asked.

"It's not coffee."

"Admit it, tea is growing on you."

"I admit no such thing!" Haley smirked and took another sip. "However, I do think this brew could be improved upon." Haley disappeared and returned shortly with a bottle filled with amber liquid. "Brandy. For our poor nerves."

Ginger lifted her cup in salute. "To our poor nerves."

Haley poured a generous amount into each of their teacups, set the bottle aside and returned to her spot on the settee. A black furry form sauntered in and approached Ginger.

"Boss! There you are. Were you sleeping this whole time?" She made room on her lap for her pet, and he jumped on. Ginger fed him one of the biscuits that Lizzie had brought in along with the tea.

"It's a dog's life," Haley said.

"He gives more than he gets, don't you boy." She nuzzled her face against his.

Ginger removed her bejewelled headband, ran her fingers through her red bob and let her head fall back. She let out a long tired sigh.

"Maybe you should go to bed, Ginger."

"Soon. I just need to unwind. If I don't, my overactive mind won't let me sleep."

"I'm the same way."

"Haley, we awoke this morning with one mystery on our hands, and now we're about to end the day with two."

"Never a dull moment at Hartigan House."

"I certainly don't remember it being so exciting here when I was a child. But perhaps that was due to my being asleep by eight p.m."

"There's the Eunice mystery and now the Turnbull mystery," Haley said. "The question is, are the two connected, or is it just terrible luck?"

"It could just be a coincidence," Ginger said.

Haley hummed. "Except for the fact that Eunice was Turnbull's guest, and now Turnbull is dead too. Both bodies found on the premises."

"Revenge?" Ginger said. "News just broke on her remains being found here. Until now, Miss Hathaway was only 'missing.'"

"True. However, the remains were found in Andrew Bailey's former room, and he's been in service with Lord Turnbull for ten years," Haley said. "And now *he's* missing."

Ginger shifted in her seat. "Yes. But that all feels too

obvious. If Bailey wanted to kill Turnbull, why do it tonight?"

"My guess would be to cast suspicion on a wider group."

"But then why flee?" Ginger said. "It only casts the light back on him."

Haley curled her shoeless feet underneath her and tugged the wool rug draped over the back of the settee onto her legs for warmth. "What about the others? Tell me how the interviews went?"

Ginger recapped the experience. "Harriet Fox is an ice queen. I remember as a young girl feeling afraid of her. Her visit to Boston was the one time I actually felt empathy for Sally."

"Is the ice queen a cold-blooded killer?"

"She denies it, of course. It *is* interesting that she was the 'replacement' for Eunice in this second soirée. I'd love to know if there's a personal connection between Miss Hathaway and Mrs. Fox."

"They would've been the same age then," Haley mused. "Maybe that's how Mrs. Fox and Lord Turnbull met."

Ginger stroked Boss as she considered Haley's statement. Her mind reverted to the interviews. "Alfred Schofield was certainly eager to leave," she said.

"Another flight response?" Haley said. "More likely he has something going on he doesn't want the police poking into."

Ginger chuckled. "The way he kept going on about his 'poor grandmother' was quite hilarious. If I didn't know better, I'd say Mrs. Schofield killed Lord Turnbull just for a night's entertainment."

Haley arched a brow. "What makes you think she didn't?"

"Mrs. Schofield is spry mentally, but physically not. We're looking for someone who is quick on their feet or has an expert sleight of hand; neither attributes can be assigned to Mrs. Schofield."

"And Lieutenant Schofield?"

"Due to his age, involvement in the Eunice Hathaway case is an impossibility, and if we work on the theory that the two incidences are connected, Alfred can't be the killer."

"I think Miss Felicia is soft on him."

Ginger groaned. "It's that obvious?"

"Uh-huh."

"What about that lawyer? He's a bit of a weasel, isn't he?"

"I'm afraid I have to agree with you," Ginger said. "I like to pride myself as a good judge of character, and I honestly don't trust the man. I wish I knew why my father did."

CHAPTER TWENTY-FIVE

"HEY, BOSSY. Want to go for a ride?"

Ginger felt guilty for all the time she'd spent away from her little Boston terrier since arriving at Hartigan House. She had particular morning errands to run and it would be more prudent to leave Boss behind, but she couldn't face leaving him in Lizzie's care for another day.

The dog wagged his stub of a tail and followed Ginger to the Daimler with the kind of joy only dogs could express. He jumped in when she opened the door. She put her handbag and Boss's leash on the floor of the passenger seat. Boss took position on the driver's side, nose out the window.

"Oh Boss, you silly man. Do you think you're going to drive? We're in London now. You need to move over to the near side."

Boss adapted easily, and soon his nose was out the window on the opposite side, lapping up the wind. Ginger drove to the City of London near St. Paul's Cathedral and found a spot for her motorcar in front of the *Daily News*. She grinned at Boss. "Are you up to a little light reading?" She clipped the dog's leash to his collar and retrieved her handbag.

The bull pen area of the *Daily News* was a frenzy of activity. There were rows of wooden desks, each with an L.C Smith & Corona portable typewriter, stacks of papers that looked precariously like they were about to topple, coffee mugs and ashtrays with smoke rising from long ashes. Several of the newer cradle telephones were in use by haggard-looking men who didn't appear to have had much sleep the night before.

A young woman with perfect skin, the latest hairstyle and a slim figure sat behind the front desk pecking away at the typewriter in front of her.

The receptionist finally noticed Ginger standing there.

"Oh, I didn't see ya."

"That's okay. It's pretty noisy in here."

"You're tellin' me. Oh! You've got a dog!"

"I hope it's all right. He's friendly."

"What's his name?"

"Boss. It's short for Boston. I've recently arrived from there."

"Are you American?"

"No, actually, I'm English, but I've been living in

Boston for the last twenty years."

"Golly. That explains your accent, then."

Ginger blinked in surprise. "My accent?"

"Yeah. You sound English enough, but there's a tinge of somethin' else." Ginger made a mental note to work on that. She had once been a master of language nuances.

"Is there somethin' you want 'ere?" the girl said.

"I'm looking for a reporter. I'm sorry, I don't have his name. He's about my height, small brown eyes, receding hairline."

"Bit of a belly on 'im, eh?"

Ginger nodded.

"Could be Mr. Blake Brown. Want me to fetch 'im for ya?"

"Please."

"Who shall I say is callin'?

"Lady Gold."

The pretty girl's blonde eyebrows jumped at the title, and she started to bob before catching herself. Ginger guessed the girl had worked in service before.

Five minutes later she returned with Blake Brown and Ginger was happy to see that he was indeed the reporter she was looking for. She extended a gloved hand.

"Mr. Brown, it's a pleasure."

Blake Brown transferred a file to his left hand then shook hers. "The pleasure, and surprise if I might add, is all mine."

"Thanks, Miss Taylor," Brown said to the receptionist, excusing her.

"I'm wondering if there's a private room in which we might have a little chat?"

"I was hoping you were going to say that. Come with me."

Blake Brown took her to an interview room and closed the door. The space was small and sparse, with only a table and four chairs.

The reporter hesitated before sitting. "Would you fancy a coffee, Lady Gold? We're all caffeine addicts here I'm afraid. An occupational hazard, you could say. I could rustle up a cup of tea if you'd prefer."

Neither offer tempted Ginger. "I'm fine. You don't mind if my dog sits in, do you?"

"It's fine by me."

Ginger patted the empty spindle-backed chair beside her and Boss climbed on.

"What is it you'd like to talk about, madam?"

"When the press were congregated outside my home, you started to ask me a question."

"Indeed. Shall I ask it again?"

"Please do."

"Did you know about Mr. Hartigan's involvement in the corporate fraud case of 1915?"

Every time Ginger's father was implicated in an alleged crime, her stomach flipped. She swallowed dryly. Now she wished she'd asked for a glass of water.

"That's quite the accusation, Mr. Brown. I'm assuming you have proof?"

Blake Brown smiled slowly. "I have my sources."

"And I have mine. My father was busy running his

American businesses in Boston and New York in 1915."

"Yes. But you have heard of this modern convenience called the telegram?"

"That doesn't prove anything."

Blake Brown put the file he'd been carrying on the table and opened it. He retrieved a well-sharpened pencil from his shirt pocket and placed it length-wise between his lips. The bite marks already present were evidence that this was a common occurrence.

Brown caught her staring and chuckled. "I'm hard on my pencils. Doctor told me I had to stop smoking—bad lungs, you see. Filthy habit bally well near killed me. Can't get away from the scent of it here. Sometimes, I just sit back in my chair and breathe in deep."

"I never picked up the habit myself."

"Good for you."

Mr. Brown was stalling. Ginger brought him back to the point.

"Proof, Mr. Brown?"

Brown pushed a file toward her. "Lord Turnbull was up to his eyeballs in bad business. It seems he convinced your late father to partner with him on one of them. Mr. Hartigan left the country and Lord Turnbull pulled strings to get himself cleared.

A dry lump of dread formed in Ginger's parched throat and she found it difficult to swallow. Had her father knowingly become involved in a fraudulent deal?

Ginger felt Blake Brown's gaze bearing down on her, no doubt trying to discern if she'd known about this.

The man chomped on his pencil, then said, "This is a

matter of public record, though it was buried deep. His lordship used his influence to hush it up."

"This is very troubling, Mr. Brown. I assure you, I never knew anything about this. My father wasn't the kind of man to break the law." Ginger's father had always been esteemed and admired by his peers. He was a good friend of the mayor of Boston, a leader among leaders in business, and though he was a wealthy man, he hadn't forgotten the less fortunate and supported several charities. Anyone who knew him would say that Mr. Hartigan was every bit the gentleman. He had impeccable manners, was certainly trustworthy, and valued integrity.

"With all due respect, madam," Brown said, "I wouldn't expect you to think ill of you father, especially now that he's gone."

Father, what were you caught up in? Proof sat on the table that he had been involved with Turnbull. He'd ordered the attic door locked with Eunice's body inside. He'd suddenly switched solicitors and hired weak-minded William Hayes. Ginger reached over to pat Boss, needing his comfort right now. With all the uncertainty surrounding her, Boss remained unchanged. He was still the same lovable, devoted, adorable beast.

"What do you want from me?" she asked.

"A story. How did Eunice Hathaway's body end up in an attic room in your house?"

Ginger folded her hands on her lap and inclined her head. "How about you and I make a deal, Mr. Brown. I'll answer your questions if you answer mine."

"One for one?"

"Okay."

"How did Eunice Hathaway's body end up in an attic room in your house?"

"I don't know."

Blake Brown tossed his molested pencil on the table. "This game won't work if you don't tell me the truth."

"I am telling you the truth. I'm looking for the answer to that question myself. I can tell you this: the room she was found in belonged to my father's former valet, Andrew Bailey."

"The same bloke who's worked for Turnbull all these years?"

"Yes. Now my turn."

"Was my father involved in any other business ventures with Lord Turnbull other than the aforementioned one, and were any of those illegal?"

"That's two questions, my lady."

Ginger pierced him with a look and Brown chuckled. "Righto. He was involved in several businesses with Lord Turnbull, but all the others were aboveboard. Believe me, I checked."

"Your turn," Ginger prompted.

"How long do you plan to stay in London?"

"*That's* your question? Truthfully, I'm not sure."

"Does it depend on how long it takes to, let's say, cover a little problem left behind by Daddy?"

Ginger's stomach twisted at the question, but she kept her expression flat. "It's my turn, Mr. Brown, but I'll be generous and answer it. Like I've already told you, this is the first I've heard of this situation." She pointed to the report in front of her. "My turn. What do you plan to do with this information?"

"If you give me a scoop, I'll make sure it's buried forever."

"You already announced the fraud outside my door. Please offer me something you actually can promise."

"I didn't finish stating the question that day, Lady Gold. Once the door closed, I let the sentence fade." He tapped the report with his pencil. "I've kept this to my chest. Reporters are very territorial over their leads." He popped his pencil back into his mouth.

"Were you aware of Lord Turnbull's latest movements?" Ginger asked.

His little brown eyes squinted to almost closed. "Last thing I heard he was attending a dinner party at Hartigan House. Last night, wasn't it? How'd that go, by the way?"

"What have you heard?"

Blake Brown sat up. "Was there something to hear? Do you have a story for me Lady Gold?"

"I do. But I can't give it to you right now."

"When, then?"

"This afternoon. Give me your number and I'll ring you."

"It has to be good, my lady. I'm not a gossip columnist."

Ginger smiled. "I think you'll be very happy, Mr. Brown."

CHAPTER TWENTY-SIX

WHEN HALEY had engaged Harriet Fox in conversation over roast mutton at the soirée, Harriet had revealed the street she lived on in Belgravia. Ginger and Boss now sat in the Daimler parked at the corner, Ginger with a set of small binoculars she used at the races and Boss with a bone Ginger had brought along for his amusement. They'd been waiting for over an hour and Ginger wished that Mrs. Fox would just get on and venture out. It was mid-morning and Ginger had bargained that after a late night drinking and watching your companion die in front of you, a lie in on Mrs. Fox's part would be merited. Maybe too much of a lie in. Or perhaps she'd already gone? Had Ginger made a mistake in visiting Blake Brown first?

If only Mrs. Fox had let the flat address slip out along

with the street name, then at least Ginger wouldn't have to use the binoculars. As it was she had to use her hat as a shield when she used them as her behaviour would cause tongues to wag and possibly encourage a neighbourhood watchdog to ring for the police. Ginger could imagine the scolding Basil Reed would give her if he knew she was shadowing one of his murder suspects.

Motorcars, motorbuses—even a tourist bus with stairs at the back leading up to the open top deck—drove by, along with the occasional horse-drawn cart. Pedestrians crossed with no apparent worry. Ginger supposed none of the vehicles were going fast enough that one couldn't dart out of the way of danger if necessary.

Ginger's attention was alerted by a strawberry-blonde woman in a yellow walking suit leaving a flat only a few yards away. Peering through her binoculars, she easily identified the person as Harriet Fox. The woman lifted a watering can and sprinkled the potted plants on her doorstep then turned in the opposite direction and walked away.

Ginger hastened to reattach her hat to her bob and then clipped the leash to Boss's collar.

"Time to go for a walk, Boss." She held a gloved finger to her lips. "You must stay quiet."

Ginger had brought along low-heeled rubber-soled shoes knowing she might have a good walk ahead of her. She slipped them on and darted after Harriet before she lost sight of her.

Harriet lived near the Piccadilly line at Knightsbridge and took the steps down to the underground. Ginger appreciated the crowds. The more people around her, the easier it was to stay close yet hidden. The train arrived and Harriet entered the front of the carriage. Ginger swooped Boss up, and tucked him under her arm, and entered the same carriage through the rear door. Now, as there was standing room only, Ginger held on to the bar overhead with her free hand. She peered around a robust gentleman. Harriet Fox sat, looking pensive.

The train rumbled on, jerking and swaying. Harriet made her way out at the next stop, Hyde Park Corner. Ginger nudged by the other passengers and followed.

Ginger stopped at the entrance of Hyde Park and purchased a copy of the *Daily News*, keeping the folded paper handy in case she needed to shield her face.

The day was warm and attracted many Londoners and tourists alike. Young and old, mothers with children, lovers strolling hand in hand, messenger boys riding swiftly on bicycles taking a shortcut to the other side of town.

Harriet sat on a bench by a fountain, set her handbag, on her lap and crossed her ankles. Her eyes focused across the greens, searching.

Definitely waiting for someone. Ginger lingered behind a food vendor, keeping herself and Boss out of sight. The sandwich man watched her then smiled and asked, "Ya want somethin' lady?"

"I do, thank you. One ham and cheese, please." Ginger had grown rather hungry, with breakfast having been consumed some hours ago. She tore off a piece for Boss, all the while keeping her eye on Harriet Fox.

Harriet's eyes suddenly widened, and a smile

stretched across her attractive face. Ginger followed the direction Harriet was looking and almost choked on a piece of ham.

Alfred Schofield had appeared from the east side of the park, a confidence in his stride. Harriet stood before he reached her, glanced over her shoulders then opened her arms for an embrace. The younger man cupped her cheeks tenderly. The passion in their kiss was unmistakable.

"Well, I'll be," Ginger muttered. How had she missed this? This couple were either particularly good at acting or had been terrified at being thrust together in front of Lord Turnbull. That was why Alfred had been so attentive to Felicia. He was using her to cover his true feelings for Lord Turnbull's companion. That tactic could very well be what had put Harriet in such a foul mood.

Their secret affair was certainly motive for murder. Perhaps they had worked together to rid themselves of a formidable obstacle to their coupling.

Ginger spotted an elderly couple resting on a bench nearby and approached them. "Excuse me. I'm Lady Gold, and I wonder if I could trouble you for a small favour?"

The couple smiled up at her with wrinkly faces. "So long as it doesn't involve running or mountain climbing, madam," the gentleman said with a twinkle in his eyes."

"Splendid, and no physical activity required on your part, I assure you. You see, I spotted a friend in the park, and she's frightfully scared of dogs." She couldn't risk Alfred recognizing her pet. As there were plenty of dog-walkers in the park, she quickly amended. "Close up, you know. Would you mind terribly watching my little dog for a few minutes? I'll just attach him to the bench."

"It would be our pleasure," the gentleman said. "What's the pup's name?"

"Boss."

"Oh, that's my wife's name, too!"

His wife pushed his arm playfully. "Blimey. Mr. Pike doesn't know how good he's got it."

"Oh I do, dear, I do."

Confident that Boss was in good hands, Ginger circled around the fountain until she was behind Alfred and Harriet, yet in earshot.

Harriet: He dressed me up like *her*. Right down to the bloody ring!

Alfred: He was a controlling devil. I'm not sorry he's dead.

Harriet: Nor am I.

Alfred: We need to be careful for a while longer, love. Until things blow over. We don't want targets on our backs.

Harriet: I just thought all this sneaking around could end now.

Alfred: Soon darling, soon.

Ginger waited until the couple left the park, then collected Boss from the pair on the bench who, not surprisingly, had grown quite fond of the little fellow in a short time. She expressed her deepest thanks, and when she walked away, she heard Mrs. Pike say, "Maybe we should get a dog, Douglas."

Ginger caught a taxicab back to her car, giving the grateful driver a generous tip for allowing Boss to travel along. She was eager to get back to Hartigan House and ring up Haley to let her in on this new development.

As she was driving down Mallowan Court, who drove up beside her than Alfred Schofield himself! He pulled to a stop in front of his grandmother's house. Instead of turning into the alley to access her garage, she parked in front of Alfred Schofield and hopped out of the Daimler.

"Lieutenant Schofield! Alfred!"

"Oh, hello there."

Ginger stepped up to Alfred with Boss on her heels. "How are you, after last night's horrid business?"

"Holding up. Terrible thing for you, though, I reckon. What a way to ruin a party!"

"Things certainly took a turn I hadn't anticipated."

Alfred stuffed his hands into his coat pocket and rolled on his heels. "Quite the beastly affair."

"Did you know Lord Turnbull?"

"Not well. We played the same tables on occasion."

"Gambling?" Ginger asked.

"Gentlemen's poker. Nothing underhanded."

"Lord Turnbull seemed like a very charming man to me."

Alfred chortled. "Yes indeed. He fooled people all the time with his charisma. I've never met a man so skilled at manipulating people. "

"Especially women, I gather?" Ginger said.

Nodding soberly, Alfred said, "Nasty fellow."

"That must be why Mrs. Fox didn't appear very upset by his sudden death."

Alfred considered her warily. "It was the shock."

"Are you acquainted with Mrs. Fox?" Ginger asked carefully. "I mean before last night's affair."

"We've met. Now if you don't mind, my grandmother is expecting me."

"Lieutenant Schofield, did you kill Lord Turnbull?"

Alfred Schofield's eyes flashed with fury. "It's true, I wanted to kill him, but I didn't. Someone got to him before I could."

CHAPTER TWENTY-SEVEN

GINGER RETURNED to the Daimler and breezed past Basil just as he parked in front of Hartigan House. She wiggled her fingers and smiled before turning down the alley to her garage.

By the time she entered through the rear of the house, Pippins had answered the front door and left the inspector waiting in the sitting room.

"Hello, Basil," Ginger said upon entering.

Basil stood when he saw her. "Good day, Ginger. I hope I haven't come at an inconvenient time?"

"Not at all." Ginger pulled off her gloves. "I was just out running a few errands."

"With Alfred Schofield?"

"You saw that, did you?" Ginger was thinking of a

way to relay her news to Basil without admitting to following Harriet, when Boss provided a diversion. He trotted over to Basil and sniffed his leg, causing the inspector to take a nervous step back.

"Have you had a bad experience with a dog before, Inspector?"

"I was bitten as a child and swore off dogs ever since."

"That really is a shame." Ginger approached Boss who continued to linger near Basil's feet. She crouched down and swooped him into her arms. "Boss is a very friendly dog. He's never bitten anyone, ever. Why don't you give him a little pat?"

Basil watched Ginger intensely. His gaze moved from her face to the dog and back. He slowly held his hand out palm down. "You're sure he won't bite."

"Absolutely positive."

Boss sniffed Basil's hand then gave it a quick lick.

"He kissed you!" Ginger, said, laughing. "See, nothing to worry about."

Basil actually smiled and moved his hand to the top of the dog's head, and patted awkwardly.

"He loves to be scratched behind the ears," Ginger said, moving her fingers to Boss's left ear. Basil stretched out his fingers to the right.

"Oh Bossy," she cooed. "What have you done to deserve all this affection?" She stroked the dog's back and then reached once again for his ear. However, Basil had switched ears, and her hand landed on top of Basil's. They both stilled then stepped back sharply.

"That's enough attention for you, Boss," Ginger said quickly, setting the animal back on the carpet. To her dismay, her heart stammered in her chest.

Basil cleared his throat and straightened his tie. "Is your staff available for questioning?" His voice cracked and he coughed in his hand to cover it up. Ginger politely ignored it.

"Yes. They knew you'd be coming. Shall I send them in? Or would you like to use my study again?"

"Here will do, Lady Gold."

Ginger sent in the first person she saw. "Lizzie, the inspector is here to speak to the staff, can you organize it for me, one of you at a time?"

Lizzie bobbed. "Yes, madam. I'll go myself, then call on the others."

"Fabulous. Where are Miss Felicia and the Dowager Lady Gold?"

"They're packing, madam."

"Packing?"

"Yes, madam. The Dowager Lady Gold says she's had enough of the big city and wants to go back to Hertfordshire immediately."

"I see. Thank you, Lizzie. You may report to the inspector now. He's in the sitting room."

Ginger found Felicia in her room in tears.

"Felicia, darling," Ginger said.

"I don't know why I'm crying. We've stayed longer than we initially planned to as it is. And though I found the events of last night perfectly screaming, they simply wore Grandmama's nerves to a thread. She's demanding we leave on the next train."

"It does feel sudden, but it's not like we'll never see each other again. I promise to visit you before I go back to Boston."

Felicia wiped her damp cheeks with a lace handkerchief. "That does bring me some consolation."

"Do you need help packing? I can send Lizzie up?" Then she remembered the staff interviews. "Or Grace."

"I'd rather do it myself. I'm not used to having other people take care of my intimate matters. Besides, I need to keep my hands busy or I'm sure to fall into despair."

"Is Grandmother packing for herself too?"

"Oh, gosh no. She got Lizzie do that for her first thing. I think she's just stewing, waiting for me to finish."

Ginger decided to leave Ambrosia alone for the moment and shut herself and Boss in her room. Her mind kept leaping back to the accidental touch of Basil's hand and the electricity that sizzled through her. She picked up the photo of Daniel and apologised.

"I'm sorry, love. It's you that I miss. The warmth of his hand reminded me of what I no longer have. I'm still devoted to you." She planted a kiss on the glass then wiped the remnant of her lipstick with a handkerchief.

Ginger studied her reflection in the mirror and reapplied her light makeup. Feeling put back together she ventured out.

Mrs. Thornton waddled out of the sitting room in a huff. "The man treats me like a common criminal!"

Ginger held in a smile. She knocked softly before peeking inside. "All clear?"

"Mrs. Thornton just left," Basil said. "I'm afraid I didn't make a very good impression. Only Mr. Pippins left to go."

"Can I ask you a quick question?" Ginger said. "I'd like to inform the press about Lord Turnbull's death before it gets out another way."

"Righto. It's best to control the angle as much as possible. I was going to call them myself once I had finished here."

"Do you mind if I do it?"

"Do you have someone in mind?"

"Blake Brown, at the *Daily News.*"

"Oh? Why Brown?"

"I owe him a favour."

Pippins knocked on the door and stepped in. "Excuse me." He made to leave, but Basil called him back. Then he turned to Ginger and said, "Go ahead and ring your man."

Ginger dialled the number Blake Brown had given her and asked Miss Taylor to connect her to Blake Brown.

"Lady Gold!" he bellowed over the background noise. "So soon?"

"I got the release to share my news a little earlier than I'd anticipated."

"Capital. Let's hear it."

Ginger relayed a shortened version of the events of the evening before and Lord Turnbull's sudden death."

Blake Brown whistled. "Consider Mr. Hartigan's file buried!"

"Thank you, Mr. Brown."

"Thank you, Lady Gold." Brown hung up and Ginger could imagine him racing back to his typewriter. He probably had time to get the story into the *Daily News* morning edition.

Ginger wondered if Basil would wait around to say goodbye or if he'd just leave when he finished with Pippins. She found him waiting.

"How did it go?" she asked, making sure to keep a polite distance between them.

"Fairly straightforward. Tell me, how well do you know your staff, Ginger?"

"I only met Lizzie on my arrival, and Grace is new as of yesterday, so I don't know them at all really. Mrs. Thornton's just newly returned to Hartigan House, but she did work here years ago. Pippins has been around for as long as I can remember. He was on loan to my father's cousin, while the house was shut."

"On loan?"

"Oh yes. Cousin Enid Hartigan was in need of a butler right around the time my father decided to close up. Very fortuitous for us all."

"Mr. Pippins left her to come back to you?"

"Sadly, cousin Enid recently passed away."

Basil squinted and Ginger could see his mind trying to process the coincidence. "It's all perfectly upright, Inspector. I trust Pippins with my life."

Before she could say more the door chimed. Ambrosia's voice bellowed up the stairwell, "Felicia! The taxicab is here!"

Ginger rushed to see Ambrosia and Felicia off.

"Pippins, do ask the taxicab driver to help with Miss Felicia's and the Dowager Lady Gold's luggage. Be sure to tell him there will be an extra tip for his efforts."

"Yes, madam."

"I'm sorry for the short notice, dear," Ambrosia said, "but I simply can't take any more excitement."

Ginger nodded with a look of understanding. "It has been uncommonly eventful."

Felicia stood beside the matronly woman with a forlorn look on her face. "I'm going to miss you, Ginger."

"Chin up, darling," Ginger said. "We'll see each other again soon."

"Can I be of assistance," Basil said as he watched the butler and taxicab driver haul suitcases down the stairs.

"I believe, that is the last of it," Ginger said. "Otherwise, we'd have to call a second taxicab just for the luggage!"

Basil placed his hat on his head. "I'll be out of your way then."

Ginger was about to say goodbye when Lizzie came rushing in. "Telephone call for the inspector, madam."

Basil raised a brow and removed his hat. "Excuse me."

Ginger hugged and kissed her in-laws good-bye. "It was so good to see you both again."

"It was much too long," Ambrosia said. "I do hope you decide to stay in London. You are family."

Ginger smiled but said nothing. She had family in Boston too. Her stepmother and half-sister. Which reminded her, she needed to write a letter to Louisa soon.

She walked with them to the gate and waved them off. "Safe travels! Ring me when you get there!"

The atmosphere inside the house was oddly still. With Ambrosia and Felicia gone and Haley at her classes, the place felt empty. Ginger thought of what she should do next. Her stomach growled reminding her that it was almost noon. She would see if Mrs. Thornton had cooked up anything for lunch.

She ran into Basil in the hall and jumped. She'd forgotten about the telephone call.

"Is everything all right?" she asked.

"It was the Yard. They've found Andrew Bailey."

CHAPTER TWENTY-EIGHT

GINGER HELPED HERSELF into the passenger seat of Basil Reed's motorcar. In a split second his look of surprise morphed to indignation then to resignation.

"I'm not sure why I'm allowing this," he muttered as he made a U-turn on Mallowan Court.

"Because I bring you luck!" Ginger said brightly. "Or if not luck, fresh eyes and objectivity."

Basil Reed grunted.

An officer guarded the door to the interrogation room where Andrew Bailey waited.

Lord Turnbull's valet wore the same serving uniform as before, but now his trousers were streaked with dirt and grime, his shirt wrinkled, and the seam of one shoulder of his jacket had split. He sat, shoulders slumped, scratching his knuckles nervously.

When Basil and Ginger entered, Andrew Bailey startled. He removed a handkerchief from his pocket and patted beads of sweat off his forehead.

"Mr. Bailey," Basil said, "I'm Chief Inspector Reed. I believe you are acquainted with Lady Gold."

Basil pulled out the first chair for Ginger and then took the seat beside her. Constable Newman stood guard by the door.

Basil cleared his throat before beginning. "Mr. Bailey. You defied direct instructions to remain at Hartigan House until everyone had a chance to make a statement. Why?"

"I-I-I don't rightly know, sir. I just panicked."

"Panicked? Are you guilty of something?"

Bailey swallowed and turned his thick neck.

"Out loud for the record, Mr. Bailey."

"N-no?"

"Did you kill Lord Turnbull?"

"No! Why would I do that? Now I'm out of a bloody job."

"Why did you leave my father to work for Lord Turnbull?" Ginger asked.

"He left me, madam, for Boston and his new American wife. He asked if I wanted to join him, but I declined. I'm not much of an adventurer. He knew he was shutting up Hartigan House and released me with references. When Lord Turnbull got wind of the news, he recruited me straightaway."

"Did you kill Eunice Hathaway, Mr. Bailey?" Basil asked.

Unlike his immediate response to the same question about Lord Turnbull, Bailey hesitated.

"Mr. Bailey, please answer the question."

"I didn't kill the young woman."

"Do you know who did?"

Andrew Bailey sighed. "I suppose there's no point in staying silent any longer. Lord Turnbull killed Miss Hathaway."

Ginger and Basil shared a look. Was this the truth, or was Bailey using Lord Turnbull as a scapegoat?

"What was the method of her death?" Basil asked. The Yard had yet to release cause of death to the press.

"He strangled her with his own two hands," Bailey said, then provided the motive. "Miss Hathaway was young and beautiful and used her charms to entice wealthy men. Lord Turnbull was easily snared by wily females. Before long he was buying her clothes and jewellery and walking out with her, despite the fact that he was newly widowed.

"Lord Turnbull claimed that Miss Hathaway was never satisfied, always wanting more. I've come to see that Lord Turnbull's relationships with these kinds of women since then were always short-lived. From what I've witnessed, his girls would weep and wail but leave on his demand. Apparently Miss Hathaway had been different. She refused to go—she wasn't about to be intimidated, she said. It's my belief that she had information she was holding over his lordship's head."

"She was blackmailing him?" Basil said.

"It would appear so. According to Lord Turnbull— he tended to confide his intimacies after a couple of drinks—she had demanded that his lordship announce their engagement. She said she didn't care if he loved her."

"She wanted the title," Ginger said. "That would've definitely given her more social standing and respect.

"Miss Hathaway had underestimated Lord Turnbull's wrath," Bailey said. "I don't know what triggered it the night of Mr. Hartigan's soirée, but the ... incident happened at Lord Turnbull's London townhouse.

"How did Miss Hathaway's body end up in your room at Hartigan House?" Basil asked.

Andrew Bailey let out another woeful sigh. "The night of the soirée was my last day with Mr. Hartigan. I was due to relocate to Lord Turnbull's residence the next morning. When I arrived, he tasked me with getting rid of the body." Bailey's eyes darkened with the memory. "I was stunned, and I started to refuse, but Lord Turnbull anticipated I'd say no, told me if I didn't help him, he'd make sure my younger brother *disappeared*.

"I said I didn't have the slightest idea how to get rid of a body. Lord Turnbull laughed, quite hysterically, you see, and then I knew the man was out of his head. He slapped his thigh and said I was to deposit the body in my room at Hartigan House and that he was sure Mr. Hartigan wouldn't mind.

"When I asked him how I was to transport the body, he said to use Mr. Hartigan's Daimler. I told him I didn't want to do that, knowing it would be bad for Mr. Hartigan."

Ginger bristled with indignation. "What did Lord Turnbull say to that?"

"He said, 'Your brother's name is James, correct?'"

Poor Andrew Bailey had done this terrible deed under duress, implicating himself and forever putting himself in the vice grip of his employer.

"We waited—with poor Miss Hathaway's body deposited in the bathtub—until we were sure Hartigan House was shut up and empty.

"I was just about to lift Miss Hathaway's body out of the bathtub when Lord Turnbull jumped up from his chair, nearly spilling his Blue Marlin. 'My ring!' he shouted. When the big bauble refused to budge over the knuckle, it was starting to swell, you see ..." Bailey swallowed. "He broke the finger."

Ginger winced at the image.

Bailey continued, "I took the body back to Hartigan House—I'd gone for the Daimler earlier—and laid it out on the floor of my old room. I parked the Daimler inside and returned the keys to the hook in the kitchen where I'd found them."

"How did you get in the house?" Ginger asked.

"There's a loose window in the cellar. It opens if you jiggle it just so."

"This doesn't look good for you, Mr. Bailey," Basil said. "You've just provided motive."

"Whatcha mean?"

"Lord Turnbull threatened to wrong your brother. He was undoubtedly hard to work for and not the type of person to give you a reference for a new job."

Bailey's eyes fluttered wildly. "I swear I didn't kill the man. I didn't kill anyone. I'm not a murderer!"

"Mr. Andrew Bailey," Basil said. "I am charging you with accessory to murder in the death of Miss Eunice Hathaway. You do not have to say anything, but it may harm your defence if you do not mention, when questioned, something which you later rely on in court. Anything you do say may be given in evidence."

Bailey sobbed as Constable Newman handcuffed him and took him away.

"I sort of feel sorry for him," Ginger said. "He really was abused by Lord Turnbull."

Basil shuffled papers on the table and slid them into a file. "Yes, well, at least we are closer to knowing what happened to Miss Hathaway."

"You don't believe Bailey's story about Lord Turnbull?"

"I think I'll let the courts decide on that," Basil said. "I now have to focus my attention on the death of Lord Turnbull."

"If Andrew Bailey's telling the truth," Ginger said, "and he didn't kill Lord Turnbull, we're back to square one."

CHAPTER TWENTY-NINE

IT WASN'T UNTIL Ginger reached the front door of the Yard that she remembered she'd got a lift with Basil and didn't have her Daimler with her. She went to the street and waved down a taxicab. The driver sat on an open-air front bench and easily reached back to open the door to the enclosed passenger area.

"London School of Medicine for Women, please," she said. "On Hunter Street."

"Yes, madam."

Ginger remembered the days before the war when the taxicab driver would have snapped the reins on a set of horses. Now he double-clutched and the engine snorted to life as it headed down Whitehall towards Saint Pancras. She had to admit it was nice to relax and enjoy the view, rather than having to engage her concentration navigating the traffic and dodging jaywalkers. Her mind was free to wander and she mulled over the facts of the case.

Eunice Hathaway left Hartigan House early in the morning of the first day of January 1914, in the company of Lord Maxwell Turnbull, a fact witnessed by many. If Bailey was to be believed, Lord Turnbull strangled her, and his first task as Lord Turnbull's new valet, was to dispose of the body.

In the meantime Hartigan House was shut up, with her father and step-mother returning the next day to Boston, the servants dismissed, and Pippins off to assist old cousin Enid.

On Lord Turnbull's instructions, Bailey returned to Hartigan House the first evening the house was shut, and on knowing how to gain access through the cellar window, took the body of Miss Hathaway and deposited her in his old attic room, locking the door behind him.

Ginger had to admit a certain brazen genius with Lord Turnbull's plan. With this crime over Bailey's head, Turnbull was in absolute control of his valet's life. A good motive for murder on Bailey's part.

With the house shut up for so long, the body remained undiscovered. The only clue that something was amiss was the telegram from her father to Pippins instructing the butler not to unlock the door to that room. This message must've come to Pippins after he left Hartigan House, but before the war began, after which time the house was shut up long-term.

Her father had given William Hayes instructions to

operate on his behalf, but Ginger didn't know what they were and Mr. Hayes wasn't talking.

So who killed Lord Turnbull? Bailey had motive, as did Harriet Fox and Alfred Schofield. They all felt trapped and controlled by the man.

When the driver parked in front of the brick building, Ginger paid him and hurried to the door. She couldn't wait to tell Haley the news about Andrew Bailey.

Miss Knight directed Ginger to a chemistry lab where Haley, decked out in a white lab coat and peering into a microscope, was in class. Ginger waved at her through the door window when Haley glanced her way and waited for her friend to meet her in the corridor.

"Ginger, is everything all right?"

"No emergencies. I didn't mean to interrupt your studies."

"It's okay. The class is ending soon anyway. In fact, I was about to head to the cafeteria after this. Do you want to join me for a late lunch?"

"That would be lovely. I'm starving."

"Just let me clean up here. Only be a minute."

Haley tidied up her station, and the two of them headed to the cafeteria. There, they collected soup and sandwiches and chose a table next to the window.

Haley watched Ginger with questioning eyes.

"Yes, I have news," Ginger said. "I just came from Scotland Yard. Andrew Bailey's been found and arrested for accessory to murder in the case of Eunice Hathaway."

"Holy mackerel!"

Ginger filled Haley in on the details she'd just gained

from the interview.

"What a strange affair," Haley said. "But why did Turnbull want to use Hartigan House to dispose of the body?"

"That's what I'd like to know. It surely doesn't look good for Father."

Haley stilled and looked Ginger in the eye. "There's no way Mr. Hartigan was involved in this."

"Then why the instruction to keep the door locked?"

"Lord Turnbull must've had something on him."

"Blackmail?" Ginger said, flabbergasted. "But what? What could be so bad that Father didn't turn to the police?"

"Maybe he meant to."

Ginger paused. "You know. He did cancel a trip to London. Just after he grew ill."

"Maybe he was too ill to travel back and set things right."

"I don't like it, Haley. Why not get his solicitor to do it for him then?" Her father's illness had lingered for several years, surely enough time for Mr. Hayes to set things right.

"Maybe the lawyer didn't know," Haley said.

"Or he did, but for some reason refused to act," Ginger said.

"Did Bailey confess to killing Lord Turnbull?"

Ginger shook her head. "He adamantly denies having anything to do with it."

"The gallows have that effect on people's memories."

They cleared up their dirty dishes and deposited them

at the appropriate counter.

"I almost forgot to tell you," Ginger said. "Ambrosia and Felicia left this morning."

"Oh, my. That was sudden."

"All the excitement was too much for Ambrosia's nerves."

"I bet Felicia wasn't too pleased."

"The way she goes on, it's pure torture to live at Bray Manor."

Haley pushed out her bottom lip, commiserating. "Poor girl. She needs a vocation. Or at least a hobby."

"I agree. Something other than attractive young men."

Ginger and Haley passed other students in the halls as they made their way back to Haley's lab.

"So we have an unhappy mistress, a disgruntled employee, and an angry lawyer," Haley said. "Which one killed Lord Turnbull?

"They all have motive and opportunity. Harriet was clearly distressed by the control he had on her. The same could be said of Bailey and Hayes." Ginger glanced at Haley. "Any word on the cause of death? Has poisoning been confirmed? Surely knowing that would point to means."

"Let's visit Dr. Watts and find out."

Dr. Watts was at a desk in a cold sterile room where the cadavers were stored. He stood when they entered, putting a hand on his creaky back. "Lady Gold! It's a pleasure to see you again."

"The pleasure's mine."

Reclaiming his seat, Dr. Watts said, "I'm assuming you've come for news on Lord Turnbull."

"That is correct."

"I can confirm that the cause of death is poisoning. I've already rung up the inspector to let him know."

"Which poison?" Ginger asked.

"That is yet to be determined. I'm going to run tests on the stomach contents this afternoon." He caught Haley's eye. "Miss Higgins, would you care to join me?"

Haley answered without hesitation. "Yes, sir."

Lee Strauss

CHAPTER THIRTY

PIPPINS GREETED GINGER at the front door.

"Pips, how do you do that?"

"It's my job to monitor the comings and goings in and around Hartigan House, madam." He grinned. "And I happened to be passing the window when the taxicab pulled to a stop." He helped her out of her coat.

"Thank you," Ginger said as she peeled off her gloves. "It's been quite a day so far."

"Can I get you anything?"

"I'm fine for now."

Pippins bowed and left her.

Hartigan House was quiet, a stark difference from when Ambrosia and Felicia had been guests, and Ginger found she missed the energy and amusement her in-laws

off

224

had brought with them.

She removed her hat, carefully repinning the hatpins, placed it on a tea table in the sitting room and then approached the kitchen. "Lizzie? Boss? Hello?"

"Lady Gold?"

The voice came from behind her and Ginger jumped. "Mrs. Thornton! You surprised me."

"Sorry, madam. I should make more noise when I walk around." The cook seemed to have appeared out of nowhere. Ginger caught the older woman's eye and searched for a note of amusement but found her unsmiling.

"I hope I didn't interrupt," Ginger said.

"Not at all. Can I get you somethin'?"

"I was going to ask Lizzie to bring me some tea."

"She's taken your doggie for a walk. The two of them seem to 'ave taken a likin' to one another."

Ginger felt a pang. Jealousy or guilt, she wasn't sure.

"Is Grace about?"

"It's her afternoon off, madam. I can brew your tea, madam. In fact, I 'ave a new one I made myself, from my own garden berries."

"That sounds delightful. Can you bring it to my room?"

"It'll be my pleasure."

Ginger smiled, but Mrs. Thornton didn't smile back. The woman has lost her joy, she thought. Yesterday's trauma was enough to blow the wind out of anyone's sails. She wasn't exactly a young woman anymore. She was in need of a holiday. Ginger would discuss it with Pippins. Perhaps Lizzie or Grace knew how to cook.

Ginger changed into a comfortable day dress, sat in her parlour chair and put her feet up. Her mind immediately went to the case, to Andrew Bailey's confession, and Lord Turnbull's death. Once they knew the exact poison, they should be able to narrow in on the killer. Haley had promised to call when she and Dr. Watts had a definitive answer.

A tap at the door was followed by Mrs. Thornton, slightly winded, carrying the tea tray. "You'll need a bit more sugar with this one," she said as she poured the tea into a cup and generously added sugar before Ginger could stop her. "It's blackberry, a wee bit on the tart side. It's good for the nerves."

"Thank you, Mrs. Thornton. Please tell Lizzie to bring Boss to me when she gets in."

"Yes, madam."

"And do listen for the telephone. I'm expecting Haley to ring me."

Ginger sipped her tea. It was a tad bitter for her liking, but she didn't want to insult the cook by saying so. "It's good, Mrs. Thornton."

The cook watched as Ginger took another sip before nodding and leaving the room.

Ginger put her head back and sighed. She'd only been in London a fortnight, and had hardly had a chance to rest. She sipped Mrs. Thornton's tea. Not her favourite, but at least it was hot.

Another tap on the door produced Pippins. "Miss Higgins rang for you, madam."

Ginger straightened, attempting to stand. A wave of

dizziness pushed her back into her chair. Her body was sending her a message. She really must rest.

Pippins stepped forward, his hand extended holding a folded piece of paper. "Miss Higgins left a message."

She opened the note and read: Atropine.

"Thank you, Pippins." Ginger's heart began racing, and she closed her eyes until it passed.

"Is everything all right, madam?"

"Yes, Pippins. I think I'm quite exhausted, that's all."

"You do look it, madam if you don't mind my saying so. Perhaps a little rest is in order?"

Ginger smiled. "I appreciate your concern, Pips. A nap is most appealing." Pippins bowed slightly before leaving, closing the door behind him.

Atropine, atropine. Ginger took another sip of her tea.

Atropine! The teacup slipped from her fingers. She jerked as the hot liquid burned through the fabric of her dress. The poison was present in the belladonna plant. Mrs. Thornton cultivated a belladonna in the garden. It had ripe black berries.

Her throat tightened, not giving her the air she needed to shout. "Pippins ..."

Ginger felt as if she were choking on her own heart. Her body flushed with heat and beads of sweat formed on her brow. Her fingers clasped at her throat as she gasped for breath. Panic gripped her mind. She was going to die.

Someone entered the room.

"G-get doc-tor."

"Oh, Lady Gold," the cook said. "Why don't you 'ave another sip of tea, eh? You'll feel better."

Mrs. Thornton picked up the teacup from the soiled carpet and refilled it. "For your dry throat." She lifted it to Ginger's lips. Ginger's mind was a swirl. She wanted relief for her thirst, but pushed it away. She stared accusingly at the cook.

Mrs. Thornton was the killer.

"Ah, you've worked it out, 'ave you?" Mrs. Thornton said as she put the poisonous brew down. "It was your own snooty dowager who 'ad me 'arvest the ripe belladonna berries. I was about to toss them out when I thought to myself they might come in 'andy, and so they did, didn't they?"

"W-Why?"

"Good question, 'why?' is. Let's go for a walk m'lady, and I'll let you in on a little yarn."

Mrs. Thornton's work in the kitchen had made her strong. She easily pulled Ginger out of her chair, braced her under her arm and forced her to walk.

"I killed 'is lordship, madam."

Cold bolts of fear ran down Ginger's spine at the woman's forthright confession of guilt.

"When I saw that red ring," Mrs. Thornton continued, "I almost passed out, I did. Same ring 'e'd given my Eunice. The cheek! Yes, madam, Eunice was my daughter."

Mrs. Thornton tugged Ginger's arm sharply and pushed her through the servants' door and lugged her up the narrow stairwell.

"When I worked for the 'Athaways, Mr. 'Athaway forced himself on me. I was pretty in those days, I was.

When I realised I was carrying a babe, I was scared to death. I wasn't married and I 'ad no money, but Mr. 'Athaway said 'e'd take care of things. I refused to have the babe torn from me. Mr. 'Athaway, 'e was angry, 'e was, but 'e went a'ead and confessed to 'is wife. She let everyone believe Eunice was 'er own daughter, but she didn't love 'er like I did. I loved 'er with all my 'eart, I did."

More steps? Ginger swayed with dizziness. Mrs. Thornton put her weight behind her to keep her from falling.

"Mrs. 'Athaway wanted me to go away," Mrs. Thornton said with laboured breath. The steps were difficult for her, too. "And that's when I came to work for Mr. 'Artigan. I was allowed to visit Eunice every Sunday, as 'elp to the nanny. My favourite day of the week, it was."

Mrs. Thornton pushed Ginger through the door at the top. Where was she? The attic?

"My 'eart almost burst with pride when I saw 'er with a *Lord*. She could've been 'appy if it weren't for the likes of your kind. She could've been Lady Turnbull. But, no. They looked down their noses at her, they did, as if my Eunice weren't good enough. And she, raised by the gentry she was!"

Ginger's legs trembled. The vision at the corner of her eyes darkened. Her lids dropped and then snapped open at a slap of pain across her cheek.

"Don't ya dare fall asleep now! Not until I'm finished my yarn, ya 'ear!" The woman adjusted her arms under Ginger's weight with a grunt.

"Now where was I? Oh, when I saw Lord Turnbull

with a new lady dressed to look just like my Eunice, I knew it was 'im who'd taken my dear girl from this world. In Mr. 'Artigan's own house! Lord Turnbull and Mr. 'Artigan were thick as thieves in those days, they were. Your father knew my Eunice was in trouble with Lord Turnbull and didn't lift a finger to 'elp 'er." Mrs. Thornton sniggered. "Eye for an eye, right? Daughter for a daughter."

Mrs. Thornton pushed Ginger into a room—a small bed, a dresser. Footprints on a dusty, wooden floor.

"You can die in the very same room they found my Eunice in. I'm gettin' my own justice now, I am."

"P-please." Ginger's fingers grasped at her throat. "Help m-me."

"This is all the 'elp you'll get from me, m' lady. Give m' love to my Eunice."

CHAPTER THIRTY-ONE

HOT. SO, HOT.

Ginger felt as if her face was about to explode. Her vision blurred and her mouth was as dry as dirt.

She crawled to the door.

Locked.

Her hands shook, red as lobsters, as she grabbed at her head. No hat. No hatpins.

Oh, no.

How was she going to escape this locked room? She scratched manically at the door. Pain shot up her fingers as her nails pulled back. She … had … to … get … OUT.

The effort exhausted her and she collapsed on the floor.

So tired.

She crawled, inching her way to the bed. The dirty floor disgusted her, the way it ripped at her stockings and made her hands filthy. She wouldn't be found dead on it.

The mattress squeaked as the small bed absorbed her weight. She shouldn't sleep, she knew this. *Must stay awake.*

She forced herself to sit up. Her throat burned as she swallowed. Barely audible, she sputtered, "Boss? Come here, boy."

In her mind she saw her beloved pet run to her and jump up. She curled up with the dirty pillow left behind by Andrew Bailey and petted it gently.

CHAPTER THIRTY-TWO

"GINGER!"

Someone was shaking her shoulders. Her head rolled from side to side with the movement, but Ginger couldn't open her eyes.

"Ginger, wake up!"

"Mummy?" Ginger mumbled. "Have you come for me?"

"She's hallucinating. Pippins! Ring the doctor. We need pilocarpine!"

"Ginger, drink this. It's water. It'll help flush the poison."

Ginger's eyes cracked open. "You're not my mum."

Haley held a glass of water to Ginger's lips. She couldn't resist. Maybe it wasn't even real, an oasis in her own desert, but she drank it anyway, feeling the cool liquid run down her chin.

Her heart pounded in her chest. "I'm ... hot."

"I know, darling. Help is on its way."

Trembling. Blackness.

"Ginger! Dr. Longden is here."

"Daddy." Tears dampened her scorched eyes. "Oh, Daddy!"

"Just drink this back, Lady Gold."

Ginger swallowed.

"Let her sleep now," the doctor said.

CHAPTER THIRTY-THREE

WHEN GINGER AWOKE it was morning. Instead of feeling refreshed and energetic, her limbs felt like heavy weights. Her eyes were dry and scratchy, her lips parched.

"Drink this."

Haley lifted Ginger's head and propped a glass of water to her lips. Ginger drank then let her head flop to her pillow.

"I feel like I've been hit by one of those red General buses."

Haley gripped her warm hand and squeezed. "I'm just..." Her voice cracked. "I'm just so grateful you're still with us."

"I'm rather glad myself."

"Dr. Longden says you're going to be fine. The

poison will work its way out of your body in a few weeks. In the meantime, you're meant to rest."

"You'll get no arguments from me. At least not today."

Ginger eyed her friend. Unlike the faux bob she usually wore, Haley's long hair was braided, a single rope that fell over her shoulders, curls escaping. Her eyes were tired with tell-tale rings of worry and fatigue.

"Did you sleep at all?" Ginger said.

"A bit. In your chair. I couldn't leave you until I knew you ..."

Ginger smiled softly. "I'm all right, Haley. I'm going to be good as new before you know it."

"I'm counting on that."

"How did you find me?" Ginger had been certain death would claim her in the attic room.

"The boss was going crazy," Haley said. "Pippins tried to settle him, but the dog continued his antics up the stairs. Pippins followed him to the attic room. When he found it locked, he used the skeleton key he always carries and opened the door."

"Oh Bossy," Ginger said. "You saved my life."

On hearing his name, the pup jumped onto the bed. Ginger patted the empty spot beside her and he curled in under her arm.

"Any word on Mrs. Thornton?" Ginger asked.

Haley shook her head. "I really don't know anything. I can call Inspector Reed if you like."

A knock on the bedroom door interrupted them, and Haley went to see who it was.

"Hello, Pippins," she said.

There was whispering in the passage so Ginger couldn't make out the words. Haley stepped back in and said, "I don't have to call the inspector. He's here."

"What?" Ginger propped herself up on one elbow but didn't have the energy to swing her legs off the bed.

"Lie back," Haley instructed. She propped pillows up against the headboard and helped Ginger to sit upright.

"Don't tell me you've invited him into my room!"

"We don't have a choice. Inspector Reed is here in an official capacity. He was eager to learn that you had woken up." Haley winked. "I think he's *especially* eager for your welfare, Lady Gold."

"Oh, pfft."

"Are you ready to see him?"

Ginger may have suffered from poisoning, but her mind wasn't so clouded that she'd forget proper presentation.

"Bring me my silk negligee, the emerald-green one," she instructed. "It's in that drawer."

Haley retrieved the item and helped Ginger into it.

"And now my makeup box."

"For pity's sake, Ginger. This is a crime interview, not a fashion shoot."

"Quite right. It's too much. Just the mascara and lip balm then."

Haley collected the items with mock indignation. "I've no doubt your health is on the rebound. Either that or you're in denial about your feelings for the inspector."

"Miss Higgins," Ginger said. "You keep forgetting

that the inspector is married."

Haley shrugged. "Yet, he's failed to produce a wife."

"You think she's a phantom? Why would the inspector pretend to be married?"

"I'm not saying he's pretending. Just that the marriage is suspect."

Ginger knew this to be true, yet she didn't want to give Haley any slack. "He wears a ring."

"Perhaps he thinks it gains him respect in the community. Or maybe it keeps unwanted female attention at bay. He *is* rather attractive."

"Hmm. I hadn't noticed." Ginger stared at her reflection in the mirror. "*Oh, mercy*. I look dreadful."

"You do not look dreadful. You look like someone who barely escaped death. Can I fetch the inspector now? I'm sure he's on pins and needles."

"Yes, all right."

Ginger, aware that fussing over her looks at a time like this was the epitome of vanity, scolded herself for it. Haley was right. This wasn't an occasion to concern herself with her appearance. A small voice accused her—*you wouldn't care so much if it were another inspector coming to interview you. Someone less dashing, perhaps.* She pushed the voice aside.

Haley returned with Basil Reed in tow. His eyes, normally unrevealing with professionalism, flashed with worry, the lines on his brow deepening. "Lady Gold, how are you?"

"Very tired, but Dr. Longden thinks I'm going to live."

Basil Reed collected himself. "Righto. Very good."

Haley sat in the chair she'd spent the night in, providing decency to the situation. It certainly wouldn't do for Ginger and the inspector to be alone in Ginger's bedroom.

Inspector Reed's eyes landed on the framed photo of Sir Daniel Gold on the night table. Ginger noted how his gaze lingered there. "My late husband," she said, declaring the obvious.

"I presumed. Is he buried in France?"

"Oh no. He's in the family plot at Bray Manor."

"Has anyone informed Dowager Lady Ambrosia and Miss Felicia of your ... of the unfortunate events which occurred yesterday?"

"I don't know. Haley?"

Haley pushed her braid over her shoulder. "Not to my knowledge."

A sense of dread crept up Ginger's spine. "Do you think they're in danger, Basil?"

"I don't believe so. As a caution, I've dispatched two constables to stand watch over Bray Manor."

Ginger let out a breath. "Thank you. And if it's not necessary to the investigation, I'd ask that they remain unaware. Ambrosia's nerves couldn't take it."

"Of course." Basil removed his notebook and pencil from the pocket of his overcoat. "I don't want to take up too much of your time. I'm sure the doctor's orders are for you to rest." He studied his notes, then stared back at Ginger. "Can you relay to me your steps exactly from when you left Scotland Yard yesterday?"

Ginger inhaled and began her story. "I took a taxicab

to the medical school. Haley and I ate together there."

"Did you discuss the case?"

"Yes. I told her about the interview with Andrew Bailey and she told me that Dr. Watts had confirmed that Lord Turnbull had been poisoned, but he had yet to identify which poison.

"From there, I took a taxicab back to Hartigan House where Mrs. Thornton offered me a cup of tea. I took it in my room because I'm comfortable here. Once I'd drunk a cup, Mrs. Thornton returned, and took me to Bailey's old room."

"Did she say anything to you?"

"Yes, indeed. A full confession." Ginger relayed Mrs. Thornton's relationship to Eunice and how she'd recognised the ring. Basil scribbled furiously in his notebook. "I wondered why she was hovering in the dining area, quite unusual for a cook. She must've noticed the similarities in the guest list. Lord Turnbull's Blue Marlin was a perfect cover for belladonna berry juice. It makes sense now, why Mrs. Thornton took biscuits into the drawing room after dinner. She needed a reason to get to the drinks trolley."

"I'll need to take the bottle of Curacao for evidence," Basil said.

Haley interjected. "I still don't understand why she went after you?"

Ginger glanced away, feeling ashamed. Her father's memory and the family name would forever be tainted by these events. "My father was involved with Lord Turnbull, I don't know how, but Mrs. Thornton considered him guilty by association. The fact that Eunice's body was found in this house lends credence to this theory."

"I think I can set your heart at rest there," Basil said. "The Yard has scoured all of Lord Turnbull's finances and business affairs. Lord Turnbull had been running a Ponzi scheme through a joint venture Mr. Hartigan had helped to finance. He had been in Boston for some years, and it appears he was unaware. According to William Hayes, he'd planned to return to London to set things right, but became too ill to travel. He'd instructed Mr. Hayes to go to the police, but Mr. Hayes believed such an action would drag the Hartigan good name through the mud."

A huge weight lifted off Ginger's shoulders at this news. Her father's reputation would remain intact, the family name unscathed. She felt a sense of gratitude for the solicitor. "He was probably right."

"Yes, however, had Mr. Hayes come to the police, Lord Turnbull would be alive."

"Is he in trouble?" Ginger asked.

"He's protected by solicitor/client privilege."

Ginger's conscience chastised her. She had misjudged the solicitor.

"Is there anything else you need, Inspector?"

Basil closed his notebook. "I think that is all for now."

Haley broke in. "Any word on Mrs. Thornton?"

"Oh, yes. I noticed one of your art pieces missing, Lady Gold, and had a wire sent to all the galleries, auction houses, and pawn shops. Mrs. Thornton was picked up in York."

"Which piece?" Ginger asked.

"The Mermaid."

CHAPTER THIRTY-FOUR

GINGER WASN'T USED to eating humble pie, but when she was wrong about something, or someone, she was the first to admit it. She faced Mr. Hayes across his massive oak desk and with genuine contrition said, "I've judged you wrongly, Mr. Hayes. For whatever reason, I immediately mistrusted you. I presumed you were cheating my father somehow and instead it turns out you were protecting him and his reputation. I'm deeply sorry for this error and if I've wounded you in any way, please accept my apology."

William Hayes tented his fingers and smiled. "You're not the first to misjudge me, Lady Gold, and you shan't be the last. I take it as a compliment, actually. In my profession it helps to keep people on their toes and guessing. So yes, apology accepted."

"Thank you."

The solicitor leaned forward and said quietly, "I should offer my own apologies to you, my lady. I cringe at the unprofessional behaviour I displayed in your home. It's a huge embarrassment, really. I'm much better suited behind a desk with a stack of papers to read and sign."

"We all deal with stressful situations differently," Ginger said. "I'm just sorry you had to experience it all."

The solicitor leaned back in his big leather chair and resumed his finger exercises. "As Nietzsche said, what doesn't kill you makes you stronger."

Ginger laughed and then stood to leave. "Good day, Mr. Hayes."

"Good day, Lady Gold."

Ginger claimed a table at a teashop on Regent Street and watched out the window for Haley to arrive. Ginger's focus moved from the pedestrians on the pavement, horse and buggies, and motor vehicles on the street to her reflection in the pane of glass.

She removed her gloves and smoothed out her bob, tightening the curls on either side so the tips landed mid-cheek. Her eyes were clear and she looked rested. Dr. Longden had declared her to be atropine-free and given her a clean bill of health. She repinned her black velvet hat. It had a left-side rolling rim with a large forward-facing royal-blue feather, and rested at a perfect angle on her head.

A moment later, Haley blew in along with a cool mid-autumn breeze.

"Hello, Nurse Higgins," Ginger said jovially. "I have

to keep calling you that while I can. Before long I'll be obliged to call you Dr. Higgins."

Haley took a seat and removed her gloves. "You can call me whatever you like, Lady Gold."

Ginger smiled fondly at her friend. Despite the simple felt cloche on Haley's head, the wind had wreaked havoc on her faux bob. Long strands of curls framed her wide face.

The waitress arrived and they placed their orders: mint tea for Ginger and strong coffee—milk and two sugars—for Haley.

"Good to see you up and about," Haley said.

"Oh, I've been busy."

Haley inclined her head. "Oh, really. Do tell."

"First of all, I've made a decision about London. I'm staying."

"That's great news!" Haley said. "I mean, I'm only saying that because I'm here. Once I go back to Boston, then I'll be sadder than a wet cat."

"You're definitely going back?"

"That was always the plan. Get my doctorate here, then go back to the States to practice. My family's there. I made them a promise."

"Yes, well, let's not get ahead of ourselves. You're here for another couple of years at least."

"At least," Haley said. Their beverages arrived and they took a moment to savour their first sips.

Ginger looked Haley in the eye and said with a note of excitement in her voice. "There's a reason I made you come to Regent Street to meet me."

"I wondered about that," Haley said.

"See that empty storefront over there." Ginger pointed to a commercial space in a four-storey building made of limestone with a "To Let" sign in the window.

"Yes?" Haley said, drawing out the word.

"It's been let. To me! I'm staying in London and I'm opening a dress shop!"

Haley set her coffee on the table as her jaw lagged. "That's perfect, Ginger!"

"I know. I need something to do, and well, I love fashion. The kernel of the idea was planted in my mind when Felicia and I were investigating the other shops. I couldn't help but think running a dress shop would be fun. The people one would meet. The clothes one could wear."

"I've no doubt that you'll be the talk of the town in no time at all," Haley said with a happy glint in her eyes. "Do you have a name picked out?"

"I do." Ginger moved an open palm through the air like a banner. "I'm calling it *Feathers & Flair.*"

THE END

MURDER AT BRAY MANOR
A Ginger Gold Mystery #3

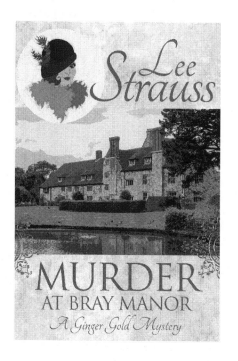

A poltergeist guilty of murder?

Ginger Gold receives a letter from her sister-in-law, Felicia, requesting Ginger come straightaway to her late husband's family home, Bray Manor. Dowager Lady Gold, Ginger's nervous grandmother through marriage, believes the old manor is haunted.

Ginger doesn't believe in ghosts, but is haunted nevertheless by memories of her husband and the lure of his gravesite she just can't bring herself to visit.

In order to keep Bray Manor afloat financially, Felicia and Ambrosia have opened the estate to the public for club meetings and special events. Knitters, stamp collectors and fly-fishers converge weekly—targets for the zeitgeist that seems to find amusement in hiding small things from their owners.

Bray Manor hosts a dance to raise money for maimed soldiers who struggle with peacetime after the Great War. Felicia invites her flapper friends *and* her new beau, Captain Smithwick, a man Ginger has met before and definitely doesn't like.

When the dance ends with the discovery of a body, Ambrosia is certain the poltergeist is to blame, but Ginger is quite sure the murderer is made of flesh and blood.

ABOUT THE AUTHOR

Lee Strauss is the author of A Nursery Rhyme Suspense, The Perception Series (young adult dystopian), and young adult historical fiction . She is the married mother of four children, and divides her time between British Columbia, Canada and Germany. When she's not writing or reading she likes to cycle and hike. She enjoys traveling (but not jet lag :0), soy lattes, red wine and dark chocolate.

Lee also writes younger YA fantasy as Elle Strauss and inspirational romance as Hope Franke Strauss.

For more info on books by Lee Strauss and her social media links visit leestraussbooks.com. To make sure you don't miss the next new release, be sure to sign up for her readers list!

BOOKS BY LEE STRAUSS

The Perception Series (YA dystopian/sci-fi/romance)
Ambition (short story prequel)
Perception (book 1)
Volition (book 2)
Contrition (book 3)

Playing with Matches (WW2 history/romance)
Playing with Matches

A Nursery Rhyme Suspense (Mystery Thriller)

Gingerbread Man
Life is but a Dream
Hickory Dickory Dock
Twinkle Little Star

Ginger Gold Mysteries (Cozy Historical)

Murder on the SS Rosa (1)
Murder at Hartigan House (2)
Murder at Bray Manor (3)

ACKNOWLEDGMENTS

Writing by nature is a solitary business — but thankfully publishing is not! Without the help of so many wonderful people, I wouldn't be able to do the work I love.

My thanks go to Angelika Offenwanger for her early read-through and making sure I got off on the right foot before too much blood had been shed; my editor Robbi Bryant for taking my words and making them shine, and for catching those problematic spots before they grew roots; my British beta/proofreader Heather Belleguelle for her super-keen eye, not only for typos, but for the small story details that make such a big difference, and for her insights on all things English - I'm so glad you reached out!

Steven Novak for rocking the cover once again!

A shout out to Debbie Sessions and her blog The Vintage Dancer for her resource and expertise on the styles of the 1920s.

I would've drowned and probably have died if it weren't for Shadi Bleiken signing up as my administrator/assistant. Alone I was a sinking ship, but together we're sailing the high seas. So thankful for you!

Special thank you to Lisa Lockwood for her suggestion of Feather and Flair for the name of Ginger's dress shop.

None of this would be worth it without the love and support of my family and friends. Big hugs and kisses to you all, especially Norm Strauss, Joel & Shadi, Levi, Jordan, and Tasia Strauss, Gene and Lucille Franke, and my gals Lori Van Zyderveld, Donna Petch, Shawn Giesbrect, and Norine Stewart.

And as always, eternal gratitude to Jesus who continually shows me unconditional love and kindness.